Egyptian Destiny: The Weight Of Her Feather

LAURA HAWKS

LAURA HAWKS

ISBN: 0997659440
ISBN-13: 978-0997659443

DEDICATION

Always for my mother, whom I miss more and more with each passing day. And to my fans, who have supported and followed me since I started this journey. You are what keeps me going and brings a smile to my face. Thank you all so much.

Please note: This story started out as a short story in an anthology. I felt I left too much out and so now that I have the rights back, I submit this to you as a novella.

On that note, I'd also like to take a moment to thank a few other special people who were part of the original anthology. So. Thank yous go out to Lori, who got me involved in the anthology to begin with. To Bryce, who worked tirelessly in putting the anthology all together and for the multitude of questions she had to answer. To Jess, who did a wonderful job of bringing the anthology together with wonderful cover work. And finally, to my fellow authors in the anthology in making the project become a reality. I hope you all enjoy my little piece of this project.

Egyptian God/Goddess Tree:

Author's Note: Some myths show Osiris and siblings were the children of Geb and Nut; others show them as the children of Ra and Nut. I've chosen the latter myths for my story. Please note there are over 2,000 Egyptian Gods and Goddesses depending on the time period and myths told of them. I've chosen the most common for this story. I hope you enjoy.

Ra: Sun God: Father of Osiris, Set, Isis, Nephthys

Osiris: God of Death, Fertility, Resurrection: Father of Horus

    Married:

Isis: Goddess of Nature, Magic, and a Protector against Evil: Mother of Horus

Apep: God of Darkness, Thunderstorms, Earthquakes and Chaos: Brother to Ra

Set: God of Chaos: Father of Anubis

    Married:

Nephthys: Goddess of the House and Mummy Wrappings. Protector for the Death Experience: Mother of Anubis

Anubis: God of Mummification, Afterlife, and Ushering Souls into Afterlife: Later adopted by Isis and Osiris

Ma'at: Goddess of Justice and Good

Bast: Cat Goddess: Goddess of the Moon, Protector against Mice, Rats and Snakes

Sekmet: Lion Goddess: Goddess of War and Healing

Neith: Goddess of War and Hunting

Thoth: Scribe of the Underworld, inventor of Egyptian writing

Ka: Soul

Chapter 1

Ancient Egypt:

Anubis squatted on the hill, leaning on his staff as he watched the procession headed toward the Valley of the Kings. The group followed the shimmering golden sarcophagus, trailing as far as the eye could see. Well, a human eye, at least. Anubis wasn't human.

The god of the dead, he greeted those who died to lead them through the underworld, where they'd be judged against the feather of Ma'at on the scales of justice. If their heart was as light as the feather, then they'd pass and proceed to the Valley of the Dead, where they'd reap the rewards of a happy afterlife. If, however, their heart was heavier than the feather, indicating their lives were harsh and unjust toward others, the god Ammit would be waiting to devour it, preventing them from attaining happiness in the underworld. Ammit was a god with the head of a crocodile, the forequarters of a lion, and the rear of a hippopotamus. The whole ceremony was presided by Osiris, the green-skinned god and overseer of the underworld. Each and every case would be brought forth to Osiris to pass the final judgment, especially if the feather weighed heavy. What were the circumstances for its weight? Were they honorable. Or, if heavy, a cause of being selfish and narcissistic? Even Ammit wouldn't make the move until Osiris decreed they wouldn't continue into a happy afterlife.

Osiris' green skin was a result of his own death. His brother, Set, had murdered him and chopped his body into many pieces, scattering them about the lands. A god of chaos, Set hated his brother and wanted Osiris's throne. Osiris's wife, Isis, searched high and low for every piece, finding all but one, which had been eaten by a fish in the Nile. She painstakingly put the pieces back together, minus the god's penis since it had been devoured by the fish. Because he was already deceased when Isis put him back together, his skin had turned olive green. As the first to die, Osiris ruled the underworld and therefore dealt with all the duties concerned with his new position.

Anubis waited for the procession to reach the newly completed tomb. He'd then meet the Pharaoh and lead him through the land of the dead to stand before Osiris, Ma'at, and Ammit. He wasn't surprised when his second, Asim, appeared at his side a moment after the religious leaders entered the enclosure.

"It is time, my lord. Osiris and the others await."

Anubis rose slowly, taking on his full, intimidating height of 7.5 feet. Asim bowed his head in respect.

"This one will take a while. His life was full, and his decrees must be thoroughly scrutinized. He undid several actions we'd established millennia ago. As my second, you'll need to answer any calls until my return."

"Of course, my lord," Asim responded, then transported to Anubis' Temple to handle any requests.

Anubis watched him disappear, smiling only

after he was gone. Asim was a good man, fighting for Anubis' causes as he was needed and giving Anubis time away from his duties on this plane in order to handle those in the realm of the dead. Asim's name meant guardian or protector and Anubis' beta lived up to the words each day since he became a were-jackal.

Thousands of years ago, Anubis decided he needed an army on earth. Well, decided might not be the right word. In 3100 BC, King Scorpion worked to unite the upper and lower areas of Egypt, repairing the division that divided the lands. It was a long, bitter battle to achieve unification. Only the strength of the Scorpion King, as well as the deals he made with the gods Re and Atum, succeeded in uniting the fractured areas. Anubis created an army to help defeat the Lower Kingdom of Gods and aid in amalgamation.

The first in his army had been Asim, a lad who was a faithful follower of the jackal god. Anubis knew he'd be a good leader and asked him to be the first of Anubis' soldiers.

Asim wasn't sure what was entailed in being one of Anubis' soldiers, but he didn't care. He was young, and full of excited exuberance at having been chosen by Anubis himself. Asim readily agreed. After all, who could say no to a god, much less their idol? At Anubis' instructions, Asim met him at the temple of the jackal god at the light of the full moon. None of the priests were around, but Asim was fine with that. There was a small part of him that prided on being selected and he didn't want to compete with others for the attention he was about to receive.

He had arrived early in heightened anticipation. He entered the temple and sat at the feet of the huge statue of Anubis'. He hadn't actually met the god, but the divine being had spoken to him through his dreams or in an ethereal form. Asim had been orphaned as a youth. He raised himself, taking what he needed and making do as best as he could. He was often envious of the families he would see in the marketplace or among the caravans that passed him by. He wished he had others who loved him and cared for him, but he was one to make the most of a bad situation, struggling for survival in any way he could.

It was during an attempt to steal food from Anubis' Temple that was left behind for offering that the jackal-headed god first noticed him. He appeared in his dreams that night. Anubis probably should've been furious with him for stealing from his temple, but instead Anubis seemed to take the lad under his wing, finding the boy resourceful. Asking Asim to be Anubis' soldier was the epitome of all Asim could ask for. The god accepted him, and although he didn't coddle him or hug him, Asim still appreciated being part of something bigger than himself.

Asim spent hours waiting until the full moon was high in the cloudless, sparkling night sky. The twinkling stars gave the night an almost dreamlike ambiance. Then, when Asim was about to give up, thinking it too late for Anubis to arrive, believing he had been forgotten yet again, the statue shook slightly and Anubis walked out of the massive granite replica.

Anubis approached Asim, his massive height making the youth feel even more insignificant than before. Sensing the boy's slight discomfort and nervousness, the god didn't wait or speak to him, but morphed into a jackal. Without giving Asim any chance to react or change his mind, the animal god pounced on him, knocking him to the ground. Standing on the boy's chest, he bit Asim on his raised arm.

Shock coursed through Asim's veins, along with adrenaline, as he struggled to get away from the god, who seemed to have gone suddenly crazy. Was Anubis trying to kill him? Was asking him to be part of his army a ruse for his demise? Was this finally payback for having stolen offerings from his temple? Did Anubis play him for a fool? A youthful imbecile who would now be punished for his audacity and disrespect?

Asim didn't know what to think as his fight for continued existence became the utmost important thought. Fight or flight, either would be preferable to this strange attack. After biting him, Anubis licked Asim's wound before jumping off and moving a safe distance from him. Asim stood, fury clearly etched on his youthful features.

Anubis once told Asim that his defiance was one of the major attractions to Anubis, one of the many things he knew would be a strength for him, and would be again once the shock wore off from the attack.

Asim stood, raising his arm up to look at the injury, the blood soaking into his tunic. "Why? Why did you attack me? I did all you have asked of me. Is this punishment?"

Anubis transformed again into his massive height. "No. It wasn't punishment. It was necessary to have you pass."

"Pass? My lord? I don't understand. This was a test?" Although Asim began to calm slightly, knowing he wasn't being killed, at least not immediately, his anger was still strong. As was his lack in understanding of the overall situation.

"Not a test, my son. I'm sorry, but it had to be done to have you cross over and be effectual in my name. I wish I could ease the pain, but I promise, it won't last. Return to my temple tomorrow. I will meet you here. You'll understand better then. I'll explain any remaining questions you have at that time."

Upon those final words, Anubis dematerialized into nothingness, leaving an astounded, shocked Asim behind. With nowhere else to go or nothing else to do, Asim left the temple and returned to the small abode he had provided for himself over the past couple of years. More of a shack than anything else, it was sufficient for his mortal needs.

That night, Asim became terribly ill. He felt as if his insides were burning as his bones rearranged themselves. A couple of miserable, sweaty hours later, Asim was no longer a man, but a jackal, his fur the color of night. It was then he understood. Anubis had turned him. He was no longer pure human, but one worthy to lead the armies of the great god.

Anubis taught him everything he needed to

know, including how to use the new abilities he had gained with the metamorphosis. Since then, Asim had grown into not only a handsome man, but also a strong, formidable warrior. Anubis couldn't be more proud or trusting of his loyal beta.

Anubis often left Asim in charge while he tended to his underworld duties. Now, seeing things were well in hand for the procession, Anubis shimmered into the world of the dead to greet the newly deceased Pharaoh and lead him to the judgment chamber and the trial that awaited him.

Asim reappeared in Anubis' Temple as a jackal. Moving stealthily to his perch where he could watch the entrance and be out of the way of the priests, he curled up to rest. He hadn't been there long when a young woman burst into the temple to launch herself at the feet of Anubis' statue in the center of the room, sobbing profusely.

Asim poked his head up. What could she possibly want? Why was this female creature so distraught?

Her head was buried against her arms, her dark hair fanned about her slim figure, but there was something else Asim felt from her. An essence, a spirit, which enticed him even though he couldn't see who she was. What was it about her that intrigued him? It was probably because one rarely came into Anubis' Temple, and when they did it certainly wasn't with extreme distraught emotion.

Several minutes of her weeping and he couldn't take it anymore. Her heartbreaking sobs were piercing his very soul. He couldn't remember a time when he heard such bemoaning. Sure, he had killed many men, even heard those wounded on the battlefield wail in painful anguish with their dying breaths. And there were even moments he heard some of the women crying for the men who perished in those battles, but he would leave the humans to their grief, for he suffered enough of his own as a child that he didn't want to bother with those of others. However, this woman whose arms spread wide over the stone figure of Anubis affected him in some way he didn't think possible. Surely there was something more he could do other than listen to her lament so mournfully.

Decision made! He materialized in his jackal form behind the statue and walked around to sit by the enormous feet of Anubis. It took her a minute to realize there was someone, or rather something, else near her. She caught her breath, wiping her eyes to look up, knowing her space was suddenly intruded upon. She was unsure if she was seeing correctly the jackal sitting so serenely by the heel of Anubis. She was uncertain whether or not she should be scared, but this was, after all, the temple of the jackal god. Was he here to help? Or was it a wayward creature taking refuge from the sun's heat?

The jackal didn't move. He sat there, his head tilted slightly as if wanting to hear what she had to say. She knew gods could read minds, but maybe in his anthropomorphic state Anubis couldn't use that ability? Or maybe, it wasn't Anubis but one of his priests? Either way, the jackal seemed more curious than anything. She wiped her eyes again, giving the animal a small smile. Slowly she held her hand out in a trusting gesture. The jackal didn't move. She realized she was being foolish. "Stupid me. You're waiting for an offering, not an empty hand."

She rummaged around in her bag slung over her shoulder and pulled out a handful of wheat and some fruit, moving to the altar to place her offerings upon it. She turned about expectantly to face the jackal, but he hadn't moved. Had she not known better, she'd almost assume the animal was a statue as well.

"I'm sorry. I can bring more back tomorrow." She became teary eyed once again, turning away to deal with her immense sorrow. "I shouldn't have come." She began to head back toward the entryway, her tiny feet dragging in grief, which radiated off her in waves.

Asim watched her. She moved with such grace and poise. He lived and dealt mostly with men. He put himself above his remaining human carnal needs, trying to set an example to the others in the army, as well as be worthy of Anubis and the needs of his Alpha God.

She was beautiful; with her soft olive skin and dark flowing hair, she took his breath away. She was petite, no more than five feet, if that. Thin, but not so much that she looked deprived of food at any time in her life. Her almond-shaped, deep brown, doe-like eyes looked almost too big for her small, heart-shaped face. Her dress was finely tailored; he could tell she was one of the privileged elite in Egyptian Society, who most likely lived with or near royalty. She touched something deep inside of him he'd never felt before, and he was unsure how to deal with it. He couldn't just watch her anymore. He was afraid she would leave and he'd never see her again. Rapidly becoming a man, he called after her, "Please don't go. Tell me your woes, child."

She virtually jumped upon hearing a human voice and turned in shocked surprise. Her eyes roamed quickly around the room, searching for the jackal that had stood beside the statue only moments before. Her red-rimmed eyes settled back on the male, gazing at him appraisingly before she answered.

He had the same stoic stance as the animal prior to his appearance, and from descriptions throughout the centuries of Anubis' second in command, she believed it was he.

He was tall, at least six feet five inches, with short dark hair and deep, penetrating, amber eyes that seemed to pierce her very soul. Just gazing at him sent shivers to places she hadn't realized were possible until now. She should run, but her feet had a totally different reaction. In moments, she found herself standing before him, looking up. It was totally clear to her. He was the jackal and she dropped to a prostrate position to give him respect.

"Don't bow to me. I'm not worthy of reverence. I'm Asim, second to Anubis. Stand and tell me your story of woe, which brings you here." His deep, commanding voice reverberated throughout the stone walls, even though it was soft.

"I'm Namire. My father, the Great Pharaoh Horemheb, crossed over to the land of the dead.

Many said he won't pass the test against Ma'at's feather and will be eaten by Ammit. He's a good man. If his heart's heavy, it's because of his deeds to help the people, despite sometimes failing."

"And what deed do you think will fail him the most?" He felt his member twitch in a need he barely recognized as he took in her physiognomy. Even her scent made him stiffen; it was all he could do to not take her, but he was in the temple of the one he followed and, no matter how much he desired her, he wouldn't disrespect Anubis. Damn, he wanted her, though, like nothing he'd desired ever before. He focused on her words, even though his eyes wanted to roam her body. Clenching his fists behind his back, he tried to appear cool and calm so as not to frighten her any more than she might already be. At least she stopped crying. He wondered how she would look with a smile. Would the small crease in her forehead evaporate as a result? *Focus on her words, not her body*, he admonished himself.

"To curb the abuses of the state government, Pharaoh reinstated regional tribunes, appointed judges, reintroduced local authorities, and divided legal power once again between Upper and Lower Egypt. The people, they whisper he went against the wishes of the gods." He was the most handsome man she'd ever beheld. He was so tall, with rich amber eyes that seared her skin, making her whole body tingle and feel more alive than she ever had before. His arms were muscular, his shoulders broad. She wondered what it would be like to be wrapped up against his hard body. His abs were ripped, leading down to a narrow waist, barely covered. His thighs were thick with muscles and he appeared to her like the most perfect specimen of man she'd ever seen. None could compare to the strength he emitted from just a brief glance. He made her feel all warm and tingly inside. On top of that, he seemed genuinely concerned about her fears with regards to her father.

Why was she here? It took a moment to regain her purpose in visiting Anubis' Temple, that her goal was her father's ka, or soul, and afterlife. Horemheb wasn't born to attain the position of Pharaoh. Instead, he had been appointed by Tutankhamun as Hereditary Prince and Chief Commander of the Armies. Pharaoh Ay came into power after Tutankhamun, but only because Horemheb was still marching on the Asias at the time of Tutankhamun's demise. The seat of power couldn't remain empty for the time it would take the news to reach Horemheb and the actual journey it would take for him to return to Egypt.

Namire was born from his first wife, Amenia, who had passed away before Horemheb even attained the throne. His second wife refused to acknowledge her very existence, and Namire didn't mind the limelight taken off her. She knew she wasn't important to her father's new position and family, so she willingly watched from afar. However, she wouldn't remain hidden and quiet when her father's soul was at risk. "No one expected the boy king to die so young. Horemheb was a commoner made Pharaoh. The people say he is unworthy of being brought in front of Osiris because of his commonality; he won't be accepted."

Asim could tell she was deeply worried about her father's afterlife. She was a good daughter, trying to make sure his ka was safe. Yet, he couldn't help himself. He needed to get closer to her. Without consciously thinking about it, Asim moved down to her and took her hands in his, peering deeply into her dark eyes. He knew he should keep his distance, but this enchanting, distraught creature, who was willing to do whatever it took for her father, fascinated him, and he couldn't resist the siren's call. He had an overwhelming need to touch her, to feel how soft her skin was, to breathe in her scent. He knew it was a ridiculous notion, but the desire was overwhelming, the need so tangible, he could think of little else. It took everything he had to concentrate on her words and not just pounce upon her. What had come over him, he had no clue, and he honestly wasn't sure how to handle all the new-found emotions raging through his suddenly hormone-active body. Good gods, he was centuries old and *now* his body decided to go through puberty?

She inhaled sharply as he neared her and softly gasped when he touched her. Her lips were a rosy color to match the slight blush to her heated cheeks. Her hands trembled within his and her knees quivered slightly. Her breath halted momentarily, and she was light headed from his nearness. She had to keep reminding herself to breathe and focus. The presence of this man affected her in ways she'd no idea were even possible.

Anubis' commander stood so close to her that

thoughts of reaching out to caress him ran through her mind. He held her hands, his thumb gently rubbing against her knuckles, and though he only held her hands, the tingles spread straight into her belly, making it quiver and flutter. She hadn't reached out to touch anyone or did anything so brazen herself, but she wasn't stupid to be unaware of what sexual activities occurred around her. Although she never cared to explore what was available behind closed curtains of a bed chamber, she was willing to give herself over to the man before her. Moisture pooled between her legs and she knew it wasn't from the heat of the day. She shifted uncomfortably, her blush deepening.

Asim caught the scent of her desire and it fueled his own. Any blood he had swiftly moved from his head down to his groin, and he moved closer to her so he could hide the protruding evidence. *Why was she here?* It took him several moments to remember. Her father, Pharaoh Horemheb. He smiled reassuringly down at her. "The Pharaoh's in good hands, Namire. Horemheb was a good king, doing what he thought was best for the people. Worry not, for I have little doubt his heart will be light."

She was relieved with the news. Tears of gratitude brimmed in her large eyes. She pulled her hands back and flung her arms around his neck. With her body pressed against his, she could feel his hardness against her hip.

Now he was embarrassed, his ears turning a slight pink. He pushed her back. He didn't have as much resolve to keep his distance with her so close.

She seemed to realize what she'd done and quickly backed away from him. She dropped to her knees and bowed low. "Forgive me for being so presumptuous. I was just overwhelmed with the news you relayed. I meant no offense."

"No offense taken." He reached down and pulled her up, then dragged her by the arm out of the temple. "However, you need to leave."

Such a strange and sudden turn of events left her confused. "Did I do something else wrong?" Her concern was palpable.

"No. You didn't do anything wrong. In fact, you've done just the opposite, and if you stay, I won't be able to deny myself the pleasures of your body any longer. You deserve respect, and you need to depart so I can give it to you."

"And if I choose to give myself to you? Would that be wrong?" She fidgeted with her tunic, knowing she was being meretricious, yet unable to prevent herself from the desire of his being so near.

Asim was stunned. Why would she give herself to him? Did she think it would secure more favor? For some reason, that upset him considerably and he growled at her, "Your father has been secured in the afterlife. You don't need to pawn for my favors."

She flinched at his harshness. "I meant no harm, and I wasn't trying to incur your favor. I was merely concerned with having displeased you in some way. I felt your desire, yet you throw me out of the temple and shove me away as if I am a leper."

Asim scrubbed his face with one hand. The

woman was unbelievable, which, of course, did nothing to curb his desire. He hadn't any clue why she affected him so, and yet her standing in front of him worried about his reactions only served to endear her to him more. Why couldn't he just walk away from her? Why was she so enticing? This beautiful creature who came to the temple to beg for assistance had captured something deep within him. He took a step back, needing the distance from her just to think.

"You didn't do anything wrong. I'm pushing you away for your own safety. Your wish has been granted, and there's nothing more I can do to aid you or your cause."

"Then why drag me away? How is my safety in danger?"

He couldn't stand it. She was driving him nuts and his manhood throbbed to the point of being excruciating beneath his tunic. He growled, letting the fierce jackal emerge, his canine teeth showing. "Because I'll devour you if you stay. You're in danger from me."

His gruffness startled her. Although she should be terrified, she wasn't. She walked away with a slow gait. He wanted to chase after her, but he focused on remaining still. When she stopped, he was concerned and started to approach, fearful she might need him for something and terrified she wouldn't. She didn't face him as she stood still, looking around the grounds as if seeing them for the first time. No one else was there. Most were still at the tomb or in town celebrating Horemheb's ascension. She turned and again he was struck by her beauty and the increasing ache in his loins resumed at full force.

"I don't want to go, and I don't think you want me to, either."

"Don't you understand? I can't keep you safe if you stay." His voice was harsh, gravelly, filled with a lustful desire he was swiftly losing control of.

"I realize the consequences of my remaining. I know what you want. What you haven't realized is I'm willing to give it to you. Take what you desire. You have my permission."

"Are you completely insane? Do you know what you're asking?"

"Yes. I do. I've always had this inner voice that's never steered me wrong, and it's screaming for me to stay here with you. If I leave, it'll be the biggest mistake of my life."

That was all it took. He transported himself in front of her and pushed her back against the exterior wall, his lips on hers, his tongue pushing to let him inside her warm mouth. His hands ravaged her breasts, squeezing them, massaging them. She didn't fight him. She wasn't scared. She gave herself to him fully, letting him take the lead in what he wanted from her. He growled, a deep inhuman rumbling within his chest, and pulled back enough to turn her so she faced the wall. He lifted the skirt of her tunic and pressed his hands against her thighs, rubbing them. With one hand, he moved his own garments aside, momentarily surprised at how engorged his erection stood. He reached down to her sex to find it dripping wet. He placed his tip against her and, in one swift move, he lifted her up and plunged deep into her sopping core. He held one arm around her hips and the other around her chest while her hands were on the wall to steady herself. He heard her cry out softly when he first plunged into her heated treasure, but he assumed it was because he was so large, and it took a moment for her to adjust to his size, a moment he didn't really give her until he was buried deep inside of her. He stood still, but only a moment, letting her body get used to him. When he felt her inner muscles clench around him, he knew she was ready and he gripped her tightly as he continued to keep her feet off the ground like some child's game of horse and chariot, thrusting with a hard, fast rhythm. He raised his head to the sky as he continued to pound into her repeatedly.

She used everything she had to keep her hands against the wall and not fall from the slightly awkward position. Although he had her body encased in his arms so tightly, she knew if she let go, he would still manage to keep her aloft. It was odd. She felt like she was almost floating as he rammed into her. Her stomach muscles clenched and loosened with each pass. She was suspended, his strength and her own bracing against the stone was all that kept her up, but she seemed to weigh nothing to him.

His growling grew louder as his need for release increased. Her own orgasm steadily and quickly approached. She felt him shudder, the warmth of his seed spilling into her body, and it set off a chain reaction in her. Her muscles tightened around his throbbing cock as she bit her lip so not cry out, fearful of attracting anybody that might have made their way to the area.

Once they were both spent, he gently lowered her to the ground, wrapping both arms around her waist to steady her. If her legs were anywhere as weak as his currently were, she'd need him just to stand. He still had her pressed against the wall as he leaned down to lick her ear, whispering into it softly, "You were wonderful. May I see you again?"

She nodded. "I'd be disappointed if you didn't."

He flipped her around then, backing up slightly for the room to do so. It was then he looked down and noticed his own tunic slightly stained and he frowned. He looked in astonishment at her. "You're unsoiled?"

"I was. You've deflowered me, but it was my choice."

"Why? Why would you do such a thing?"

"I told you. Something told me I needed to make the connection to you."

"I'd have been gentler, not just taken you here out in the open," he grumbled, looking around as he talked. He was inexperienced himself, but he certainly wouldn't have been so crude had he known her situation.

"You're Anubis' second, able to turn from man to beast and back again easily. You've made a name for yourself as commander of Anubis' armies. I'm honored you're the one who deflowered me."

Asim scrubbed his face again. Grabbing her wrist, he dematerialized to his home. It wasn't much, but he didn't need a lot. Most days he roamed the area as a jackal or slept in the temple, keeping guard. But he had been born human and part of him would always remain so. He opened the door and ushered her inside.

"I'm sorry it's a mess. I don't have company. Ever. Sit." Asim was at a total loss about what he should do. She acted as if giving her virginity away were an everyday event. "What do you want?"

Namire was rather surprised his abode wasn't more elaborate. He may not be a true god, but he should have more than this for his service to Anubis. Did the mighty god not share his spoils from worship? Was the god so heartless as to let his best aide go unrewarded?

She looked around the sparse room and sat on the small chair when he commanded. She knew the kind of man he was from the stories that circulated about him for centuries. She'd always been fascinated by the legends that were told to children about him. She'd grown up with those stories, wondered if they were true, dreamt of him, and when she met him, she had known almost immediately who he was. How could she refuse him when he appeared before her and she got to meet the hero of her childhood dreams? A part of her realized she'd remained pure because there wasn't anyone who could compare to him.

In his presence she could tell he didn't trust her. How could she explain she'd always had a crush on him? How could she tell him she had been waiting for him her entire life? How could she make him understand she thought he was the most wonderful creature alive? She wouldn't believe her own explanations; how could she expect him to? Yet, there he was—tall, proud, handsome—pacing in front of her, demanding to know what she wanted from him.

She shook her head. "I desire nothing from you, my lord. Only to have pleased you, if but for a moment."

"What am I supposed to do with you now? Do you think because we had sex, I'm to marry you? Take care of you? What? You realize you have ruined your chances for attaining a good price for your marriage?"

"I've chosen not to marry, my lord. It's not my destiny. My heart wouldn't accept a false husband, for that's all he'd be to me."

He stopped and scowled at her. "What are you trying to tell me? You're in love with someone who can't be your husband?"

She nodded. "Yes, my lord."

"Then why the fuck would you... By the heavens, are you thinking you're in love with me? Is that why you gave yourself to me?" His intense gaze pierced her very soul. Why would she give herself to a dog? A mongrel servant who could offer her nothing?

She averted her eyes. "None compare to you, my lord."

"Explain yourself. Help me to understand. Do you think because I am beta to Anubis' I'd give you wealth and prestige to make up for what you couldn't achieve with your father?" Asim was at a loss and filled with anger at being used.

"No. I have no desire for wealth or prestige. I

prefer not being at the forefront of the people and have no ambitions to be anything other than what I am. That said, are you aware you're a legend? That stories of your exploits have been told to children for millennia?"

He thought her questions odd, but shook his head. "I had an inkling, but only insofar as being a commander for Anubis. My exploits, as you call them, are minimal at best."

"You're wrong. Your adventures of heroism and loyalty, of your prowess and kindness, have been tales told for ages. A man, born human, gave up his humanity to serve Anubis, to be his second, to stand by his side. You've been the stories legends are made of."

"I don't understand where this is going."

"I'm trying to answer your question, my lord. You wished to know why I gave my pureness to you. You wished to know why I find fault in so many others that I don't agree to have as a husband. It's because I grew up on those stories. They were my favorite, and when I became an adult, I compared everyone to you. You're what I've looked for. You're what I've wanted in my life. If I could only have one moment with you, I was going to give you everything I had. I have a finite life, but the memory of this day shall live with me forever. I've given you something no one else can ever have, and that, too, will remain with me until my dying breath. And when I do die, the weight of my heart from happiness will be lighter than Ma'at's feather."

Asim was astonished. He didn't know whether

to be embarrassed, flattered, annoyed, or flabbergasted. Namire took his stunned quietness as an opportunity to stand and move in front of him. She had to tilt her head back to gaze into his eyes. Hesitantly, she laid her hand on his bare chest. "You're all I've ever dreamed about. To me, you're the best male, and all others pale in comparison. I could ask for nothing more than to be part of your life, even for just a brief encounter such as this. I ask for nothing more. I'd gladly have left, never to be seen again, but you stopped me. I don't regret what I gave to you. I never will." She pulled her hand back and lowered her head. "I'm willing to leave now and never approach your threshold, should you so desire it."

Asim almost growled at the thought of her walking away, as if he could just use her and toss her aside like some old rag with nary a second thought. Then, in a blinking instant, he realized he didn't want her to leave. Ever. It wasn't just his having taken something from her she gave to no other, nor that she was willing to remain if he so desired. It was more than that. From the moment he saw her in the temple, he desired her. Yes, physically, but more than lust ran through his veins. Seeing her now—brave, yet fearful of his reaction—endeared her to him. Remembering how good she felt encasing his cock made him want her again. "No." The word surprised even him. He hadn't realized how strongly he didn't want her to go. "No."

She stepped back, immensely disheartened by his refusal, but stopped when he grabbed her hand

and held it gently.

"No. I don't want you to go. I realize this is a hovel compared to what you deserve, but I'd like you to make this your home, if you're so inclined." He was unsure. The last time he remembered being this nervous about anything was agreeing to allow Anubis to change him and become his beta, his second. She gave him the same timorous feelings. He didn't want to let her go, and yet, he was afraid she wouldn't stay.

She smiled up at him. "I'd like that." She looked around. "A woman's touch is all that's needed to feel homey. I'd need to get a few things from my home and let others know I'll not be returning. I'd hate to worry any who might otherwise miss my absence; albeit, I'm unsure of who would notice. Would that be acceptable? For me to go home and get a few of my things before I move here?"

"Yes, that would be acceptable. I'll bring you back to the temple and wait for you there. Get whatever you wish and return to me."

Asim waited at the temple for Namire to return. He shifted into a jackal, lying on the stone slab near the feet of Anubis' statue. The coolness of the stone always felt good against his body, especially when the sun was high, as it was becoming. He couldn't believe how much had happened in just a few hours. The sun had barely been birthed from between the legs of Nut when the Pharaoh's procession snaked around the path to his tomb. By mid-morning he had met a woman who intrigued him as no other had. Now the sun was climbing to the halfway point of the day and he was emotionally, and heat, exhausted. He let his eyes drift closed, his ears listening for her return. She said she wouldn't be long, and he was anxious to spend more time with her, especially to make up for his insensitivity of the earlier act of sex. He had just been so overwhelmed with his desire, he couldn't consider taking his time. His need was too great and all he could think of was pounding himself inside her repeatedly until they both came. No foreplay, no tenderness. There hadn't been time for that. Knowing he would have the opportunity to correct the speed of his act, he fantasized about exploring every inch of her luscious skin, of licking every part of her soft flesh, of taking his time to taste every part of her and drink of her delectable juices. He still had his duties, but he'd manage having her in his life and not make her feel neglected. He would show her how much she meant to him. He would've laughed if anyone told him there was such a thing as love at first sight, but he was a true believer now. He couldn't stop thinking about things he wanted to do with and to her, about being with her every day for years to come.

He felt the shift in the air and it woke him. He'd not even realized he'd fallen asleep, but the sun had set and Anubis was before him. He sat up, shifting quickly to face his mentor, his friend. A part of him worried when he realized he had slept and so much time passed, yet Namire had not returned. He pushed the thought out of his mind. If

Anubis was before him, then he had need for his services or he'd relinquish Asim to his own devices. Asim hoped it was the latter as he wanted to track down Namire.

"My lord. I didn't expect you. Did the trial go well?"

Anubis frowned and placed a hand on Asim's shoulder. "Horemheb went well, but I came here with sad tidings."

Asim couldn't remember ever seeing Anubis in such a mood. He looked anxious, sorrowful, and sympathetic. It confused him at first, then scared him. Namire hadn't returned, but Anubis was by his side with emotions he hadn't witnessed from him before.

"Namire?" His voice was more of a croak, his eyes beseeching Anubis to say his sudden fears were unwarranted.

"I'm sorry, my friend. She refused to be tried until I swore to tell you what occurred when she returned to the village. She apologized profusely that she wouldn't be able to return to you or have the life you two briefly discussed. She wanted you to know she desired to be with you more than life itself. She instructed me to say she died with a heart lighter than Ma'at's feather because her deepest fantasy had come true because of you."

Asim's eyes roamed all over the temple as his mind tried to comprehend such a sudden loss. Nothing made sense. He had just met the woman, and now she was gone. What was he supposed to do with that? "What? Tell me what happened."

"She was stoned. The villagers noticed she was

a bit disarrayed, and when they questioned her, they realized she had given up her flower out of wedlock, and worse, on the day of her father's funeral procession. They considered it a heinous crime and punished her. Even now, the villagers refuse her a proper burial believing she disrespected her father and all the gods because of her infidelity."

Asim looked ashamed as he sank to the floor. "It's my fault. She was so full of life and because of me…"

"No. Not because of you. They were needing an outlet for their own grief and Namire suited them for that responsibility. I'm very sorry. I know you are grieved by her being stolen so suddenly from you and just after you met her. But know this, Asim, although she's walking in the valley of the dead, she has a very light heart. She'll be reincarnated and you two will find each other again. You have my promise on this."

Chapter 2

Present Day:

Ma'at screamed as she ran to Osiris' chambers, pounding on the door. Osiris gave an apologetic look to his wife, Isis, before he stomped towards the intrusive knocking. He flung the wooden barrier wide and scowled at the goddess. He didn't like to be disturbed, and he didn't want to deal with any more trials now, especially when he was enjoying his down time with his beautiful, raven-haired wife.

"What's all the commotion about this time, Ma'at?" He folded his arms across his chest. She always seemed to bother him about some trivial molehill, turning it into a gigantic mountain because if she knew about it, it was her problem to deal with. Of course, that meant running to him and disturbing his peaceful solitude.

"It's gone! Someone stole it!" Her breath was labored from her panic.

Osiris raised his eyebrow. "What's missing? Maybe whatever it is was just misplaced?"

She shook her head. "No. It's not misplaced. It's been stolen!" she exclaimed in consternation. She knew he wasn't taking her seriously. Albeit, she wasn't explaining things very well. She took a breath, trying to calm down. "It's not where I left it. It's not where it belongs. Don't you comprehend the enormity of it all?"

Osiris growled at her. "No. I don't. Mostly because you haven't explained what the hell is missing to begin with."

"My feather."

Those simple words changed his entire demeanor. The immense gravity of the situation made itself immediately known with just those two words. Ma'at's feather was more than just some ostrich plume plucked from a flightless bird. It was the barrier that kept chaos at bay. Ma'at was the goddess of justice and good. Without the feather, chaos and disharmony would reign. Worse, if the feather wasn't found and returned to her possession within two weeks, Ma'at and everything she represented would wither and die. Humans thought it was bad now, they had no idea how horrible it could get.

"Go back to your chamber. I'll send Anubis to meet you there. We will find it. We must!" Osiris turned back to Isis, who had moved to stand behind him when she realized the severity of this loss.

Once they were alone, Isis added, "We should also call Ra. As god of the sun, as well as the brother of Apep, he should be aware of the possible negative outcome of this theft. If we are unable to retrieve it quickly, others will benefit, and others will suffer."

Osiris rubbed his face. He knew his beautiful wife was correct, but he wanted to deal with Anubis first. "One thing at a time, my flower. My own brother, Set, could be behind this as easily as it could be Apep. They are both gods of chaos. Even though Apep is also darkness and earthquakes, his fights with his brother, Ra, are legendary on a daily basis, even in this day and age. Once Anubis is dispatched to find the culprit and the feather, I'll call a meeting of those who might be affected the most." He leaned over and kissed his wife, then prepared for what needed to be done, glad he had Isis by his side.

Lyra Mayet moved to the tent and grabbed the bottle of water, taking the cap off. She used the back of her hand to wipe the sweat from her forehead, brushing her errant strands of auburn hair aside before taking a long drink. The sun was beating down on the Egyptian desert where her dig was located. Peering at her watch, she hadn't realized that her "one more moment" had turned into a couple of hours. It was worth it, though. She'd uncovered a side chamber of Horemheb's tomb, just as she predicted, despite all the naysayers and doubters. She would prove to all those in her field she was right. All those who laughed at her would see how wrong they were to judge her work so critically. She wasn't the fool they thought. She was correct in her theories and now she had validated all her assumptions. Horemheb had a daughter from his first wife, and that said daughter was entombed beside her father. The Pharaoh wasn't childless, as many believed.

She plopped on her cot, her arm over her dark brown eyes. The work would be much better at night, but her visa to dig expired tomorrow morning and they'd only discovered the entrance into the daughter's tomb yesterday. There was an immense amount to do, a lot to catalog, and they could only complete so much before the Egyptian Ministers of Antiquities arrived to make sure none of their treasures were removed or, in their minds, stolen before they were properly catalogued. She couldn't blame their caution, since many of Egypt's treasures had been removed in the early twentieth century by private collectors who thought it fashionable to own discoveries from those ancient times. Had the Egyptian Ministry of Antiquities not stepped in, there wouldn't be anything left, and a good deal of their history would've been lost for eternity.

Her assistant and friend, Sebastian Mattis, peeked into her tent through the tied-back flap. "They're here."

She sighed and sat up. "Thanks. I'll be out in a moment."

Lyra grabbed her brush and undid her pony tail to run the bristles through her long hair, trying to get it to behave a bit before tying it up again. She finished her water and put the plastic bottle in a bin she designated for recycling purposes. She hoped it was Ahmad who had come to check on them and not Paulette. The latter was unforgiving in many respects and made Lyra feel as if she were guilty of some crime.

Sebastian seemed to know what she was thinking, answering her unspoken question. "Ahmad and Paulette are together."

Lyra rolled her eyes. "Great. That's just peachy perfect." She headed out of the tent, sucking it up and plastering a smile on her face as she approached them, her hand extended in greeting. "Welcome. Welcome."

"We heard you found something?" Paulette was petite. Wrapped in a head scarf and wearing an extremely professional, skirted business suit, she was a major powerhouse in the E.M.A. She even made Sebastian nervous with her austere presence. She was a no-nonsense businesswoman in one of the higher echelons of the Ministry. She rarely came out to the sites, preferring to handle the business end of the paperwork in her office. For her to have come in person spoke volumes about the find.

"Yes. We found it yesterday, as you know. We called your office immediately. I'm so glad you came personally to examine it. You'll be very excited to see the discovery. There are only a few hieroglyphs in her chamber. It looks as if it were constructed rather quickly and almost haphazardly, but it is definitely Namire's final resting place."

Ahmad stepped up. His dark eyes could barely be seen under his wide-brimmed hat. If not for his dark skin and business suit, one would think he was a tourist. His leathery face shadowed, Lyra knew under the hat the man was bald. He was tall compared to his companion, who only measured an even 5' compared to his 5'7". "Congratulations. You must be very excited."

"We all are," Sebastian interjected. "It proves all of Lyra's theories."

Paulette gave one brief nod, a stern expression glued onto her aged face. She pulled out a flashlight and switched it on. "Lead the way." She was one of few words, that was obvious.

Lyra moved to the front of the foursome and led them through Horemheb's tomb to the rear chamber. A small door had been accessed through the stone wall leading to the hidden chamber. She had to crawl through it to get in. The others followed. The one lantern she'd left lit was still inside and she quickly moved to illuminate the darkened space with several others she'd left there for just such a purpose.

Whereas Horemheb had gorgeous reliefs on the walls of his final resting place, Namire had the bare minimum. A cartouche showed her name. A couple of books of the dead were also displayed. There were some small funerary vases of her relation to Horemheb, the four canopic jars which contained the lungs, liver, stomach and intestines respectively and, of course, the sarcophagus. The chamber itself, was directly opposite the Pharaoh's second wife, Mutnedjmet.

Paulette pulled out a tablet of paper from her purse and made some notes. Lyra stood quietly as the woman looked around at everything, jotting down whatever she saw. After what seemed like an eternity, Paulette headed back outside with nary a word. Lyra looked at Ahmad questioningly, but he just shrugged, following his superior out. Lyra turned off the lanterns, save one, and followed them. Sebastian was already talking to Paulette, who was giving him instructions. They could take their find back to Chicago and the Field Museum for documentation, as well as dating, with the standard precautions and time limitations. All the pieces would then have to be catalogued, forms sent continuously, and everything returned to Egypt after two years.

As Lyra approached, Ahmad smiled at her, letting her know subtly that everything was good to go. They'd be able to make their deadline, and she'd be bringing back some valuable historical items she could take her time with to work her thesis properly.

Once Paulette left, leaving Ahmad to oversee the packaging and inventory of items removed from the tomb, Lyra had Sebastian get the packing materials ready. It was tedious, but everything was recorded, wrapped carefully, boxed, and labeled. Ahmad would see that every piece was shipped appropriately. Extra care needed to be taken for artifacts such as these.

Lyra and Sebastian would meet the shipment in New York, then take the train back to Chicago once it cleared the specialized antiquities office and customs. Ahmad would make sure she had all the appropriate paperwork, as well, so the process would go as smoothly as possible.

The three of them worked tirelessly to get everything ready by morning the following day. The forms alone took forever to fill out and there had to be one for each piece. Vases, the mummified remains of the young woman, a few shabti (servants for the dead in the afterlife), and the four canopic jars that held her stomach, intestines, lungs, and liver respectively. There were also a couple pieces of gold entombed with her. A mirror, a pair of gold earrings, a couple of collar necklaces, a few statues and a very ornate box, which they would open later, when the conditions were right and all precautions taken to make it safe.

Their gear was packed up. Lyra entered the now-empty chamber one more time and looked around. "Who were you really, Namire? What happened to you? I'll find out. I swear, and your story will be told. I'll make sure of it. You won't be in oblivion any longer. I've proof you existed and I'm going to spread your story to the world. You won't be an unknown woman, not any more. Hell, you might even be more famous than your father. Wouldn't that just be ironic?"

Yeah, she was talking to herself, but the whole experience was giving her a sense of importance that she'd never encountered before.

"Come on, Lyra. We're going to miss our flights if you keep pussyfooting around in there. There's nothing left. It'll be waiting for us in the States." Sebastian watched the rest of the trucks depart the campsite, a cloud of dust following the moving vehicles.

Lyra crawled out of the tomb and extinguished the last lantern. "I was just saying goodbye."

"You're so weird sometimes." Sebastian had been working with Lyra since college and was one of the few who believed her theories outright. A good-looking man with sandy blond hair that hung to his shoulders and was kept in a disturbingly perfect ponytail, he could've been a model as far as she was concerned. They'd tried dating once, but realized quickly they made better friends and colleagues than anything more.

"Do you have the manifest?"

"It's in the truck waiting for you. Figured I wouldn't get you in the cab otherwise."

"Bas, you know me too well. Sometimes it's almost scary."

He laughed. "Only because you have the weirdest imagination. Especially of curses and other stuff. I'm so glad you felt there was no curse to this tomb. I really didn't want to deal with that on top of everything else."

"No. No curses. Just my career in the balance. If I hadn't found her, I would've been ridiculed even more. This find gives credence to me and my theories."

"I know, babe. You're right and now you've got the proof. I called the Field and let them know what to expect. They're getting a clean room and storage area set up for us. It'll be ready when we get there."

"Thanks for taking the train with me."

"It'd be easier to just fly all the way."

"You're lucky I didn't insist on a ship to take us to New York. It'd just take too long, but you know how I feel about flying. I'll manage this flight, but then, get me back to being a bit more comfortable with the train to Chicago."

"I appreciate your sacrifice in flying. I know how much you hate it. Ever since you lost your parents, flying has been hard for you. You know you can always hold onto me in the meantime."

"I have." She chuckled. "I worry you won't have any circulation left by the time we land."

"No worries there, babe. I work out just to be sure I survive these traumatic moments of yours."

"I'm not too bad, am I, Bas?"

He patted her head like he would a child. A part of him would always care for her in a way he was sure no other ever could. He wished they could make a go of it, but he knew they couldn't, no matter how often they tried. "No, Lyra. You're not bad. I'm used to your quirkiness by now. It's actually endearing."

"You're so good to me, Bas. I sometimes don't know what I'd do without you."

Sebastian turned to her, gripping her upper arm to have her face him. "You know I'll always be here for you. I know we're never going to have the couple kind of relationship, but you mean the world to me. That'll never change."

Impulsively, she hugged him tight. "I'm very grateful for your friendship. There are times I don't know how I'd get through some days without you by my side."

Bas stayed quiet as he held her. He was well aware of what she'd gone through the past couple of years. He'd met her as they were both finishing up their PhDs in Egyptology and Archeology. They had become study partners and he'd quickly been smitten by her. They were dating when, a few months later, 9/11 happened. They had planned on catching a taxi to the World Trade Center's Windows on the World restaurant to rendezvous with her parents, him meeting them for the first time. They were visiting from Chicago and had been anxious to meet their daughter's new boyfriend. Lyra and Bas were running a bit late for their 8:45 breakfast appointment when American Airlines' Flight 11 crashed into the Northern Tower where the restaurant was located.

Lyra and Bas had been doing some work in New York for the Met in order to finish up their degrees and she was so excited to show Bas off to her parents. They were going to make it a mini-vacation with plans to do a couple of Broadway shows, going to the top of the Empire State Building, and even taking the Circle Line Cruise around Manhattan Island. If time permitted, they were even going to visit the Statue of Liberty and trace their ancestral backgrounds on Ellis Island. So much had been planned to see and do. How unreal that in a span of just minutes her elation and excitement changed to one of disbelief, horror, and despair. As they were about to head out to the Windows on the World, they heard the disastrous news.

Sebastian was just about to turn off the television set when the broadcast was interrupted to show the first plane as it rammed into the building. Glued to the television in horrific disbelief, he sat holding Lyra, intensely watching every moment and unsure it was truly happening, all the while holding their breaths as they watched the heinous atrocities play out before them, unable to do anything but stare in shock. Along with the rest of the country, they watched in horror as people jumped from the buildings, preferring to take their own lives than to be burned to death. It was better to be able to control their own fate, even if it was to the point of choosing when and how to die. He was positive some announcer would come on and say it was all a misunderstanding, a mistake, like they did with the first production of *The War of the Worlds* when it originally aired on radio in 1939. Only after panic had set in did the people later find out it was a show and not an actual event. A part of Bas was unsure the planes smashing head first into the World Trade Towers was what was happening. It had to be some cruel joke. This couldn't be real, but it was. All too real, and it devastated Lyra. Had they been at the restaurant on time, they too would've been trapped on the upper floors as countless others were from the plane smashing into the side of the building. 102 minutes after the American Airlines' plane hit the structure, any chance of her parents escaping alive disappeared as the steel structure melted from the impact and subsequent fire, collapsing into a billow of smoke and ash that covered several blocks of Manhattan.

The events that brought the country, the world even, to its knees took its toll on everyone. So many were affected by the towers falling, the destruction of a portion of the Pentagon, and those who gave their lives to crash in the fields of Pennsylvania that Lyra's personal loss was just one in a sea of despair, with little to look forward to beyond the hopelessness that pervaded the atmosphere of those patrolling the areas of New York in a desperate desire to find loved ones alive, and confused as to who could have done such a terrible act against innocents who had nothing to do with their political or religious agenda. He, himself, was on the streets of New York with her as she posted flyers of her parents in some vain hope they had survived the destruction of the planes crashing into the buildings. That, by some miracle, they'd made it out of the restaurant to find the stairs that would lead them out of the building before the building gave way to their demise. So many bodies weren't found, only fragments, which couldn't be identified. As a result, Lyra held out hope, a hope that eventually dissolved over time.

The loss of her family on 9/11 devastated her. She felt alone, her family now gone, and if not for him, he wondered if she would've given up and tried suicide. The changes in her were extreme at times. She became sullen, depressed, listless. She was just so vulnerable, and he ached to help her in any way he could. But it was those changes that separated them, and even he wasn't exactly sure why. Maybe they were too much alike, or maybe they just weren't the other half of their soul. Either way, they realized after a couple of months after the event they were not romantically inclined, so they had broken up.

Just because they were not together in an official couple's kind of way didn't mean he left her. He still cared deeply about her and hoped maybe the old Lyra would eventually return. When the ridicule of her colleagues began, he was even more determined to stand by her side. He had seen her work, and it was one of the few things that got her out of her depression. Plus, the hypothesis was sound, even though others didn't believe in her. She soon found herself alone with few to stand by her. He knew it was hard on her and he did everything he could to help her through it all, even pushing for the grant that allowed the expedition to find Namire's tomb and proving to everyone she was not insane in her hypothesis.

Bas let her go, urging her to get into the truck

so they could head to the airport.

Unbeknownst to them both, a jackal sat on the hillside watching them. Asim arrived at the tomb too late, as everything inside had been packed and already shipped. Only this couple had remained, and he was determined to follow them both to obtain the object he had been assigned to find. The feather had only been missing for four days, and he had been put on its trail almost immediately. That left him with just over one week to return it to Ma'at or lose the battle to chaos. Anubis and the other gods were tracking down who actually took it from the secret location within Ma'at's temple and had the ability to hide it in the tomb. Who knew the tomb was being excavated and the feather would be found, conveniently delivered into the hands humans? Once they found whoever actually stole it, the gods would deal with the perpetrator. If, however, he didn't accomplish his mission in time, it wouldn't matter who pilfered the goddess's feather. Judging of the dead ceased the moment it was taken. The souls of the deceased would continue to build, as would their impatience. Soon nothing would be able to contain them from overflowing and causing havoc in the underworld. The dissension of the dead would only be the beginning of total chaos, having it overflow into the world of the living. Humans were just not ready to have the dead, the gods, and themselves intermix.

How devious was the thief to hide the feather in Namire's tomb? Memories flooded him just being here in the area. He had tried to move past Namire, to live without her in his life. A brief moment they were together, and their future was stolen in the blink of an eye. He shook off the nostalgia. He needed to focus on fulfilling his mission. He'd indulge in his memories at a later time when it wouldn't affect the entire world. He continued to watch the couple climb into a truck and drive off. Just before they were out of sight, the jackal dematerialized.

Chapter 3

Bas and Lyra climbed the narrow, steep stairs to board Amtrak's Lake Shore Limited. It was the train that went from New York City to Chicago, with frequent stops in between. Thanks to their employers, the Field Museum, they were each able to afford one of the family cabins next door to each other, which offered more space than the smaller roomettes, able to accommodate four people instead of two. Both Bas and Lyra preferred the larger accommodations to move around in.

Lyra enjoyed train travel. It was reminiscent of traveling at the turn of the twentieth century, when life was slower paced and people socialized more. Dining on the train was a communal experience, being paired up with three or four of one's fellow passengers to make up the table complement. If one sat in coach, the seat partner, or those also in the cabin, would be who you would talk to and get to know. In the more private roomettes and sleepers, one didn't have quite that opportunity, but it was also nice to have quiet, peaceful time to repose and relax. Dining would then be the time to socialize.

Once Lyra settled into her room, she laid back and stretched her feet out. She was so thankful to be off the plane, but the drugs she took to calm her nerves enough just to get on it still flowed within her body, making her a bit fuzzy headed and tired. She shut her eyes, not even bothering to open them again when there was a knock on her door. She knew it was either the conductor, the room steward, or Bas. Either way, she didn't care.

"Come in."

Bas slid the door open, stepping inside. "I brought your bag. Need anything else?"

She shook her head, peering over at him as she did so. "Thanks. I think I'm going to get some rest, then work on the reports. We should be in Chicago by mid-morning, and I would like to have as much prepared ahead of time as possible."

"All right. I'm going to head over to the bar to get some drinks. If you need me, I'll either be in my room or in the cafe car."

"I should be okay, but when you come back, can you bring me a red wine, please?"

"Sure. I'll see you later." Bas closed the sliding door as he left, affording her privacy.

The train lurched as it pulled out of Penn Station. The bag Bas had brought to her rolled over and something solid bumped against the wall. Lyra opened her eyes again, curious as to what she had in her bag that might be so heavy as to cause such a distinct thud. Reluctantly, she stood to retrieve the bag and put it on the seat beside her, opening it up. Rummaging through her clothes and personal items, she pulled out a statue and gasped in disbelief. It was a two-foot statue of a seated jackal. She had no idea how it got in her bag, and she was surprised that she had gotten through customs with it in her possession. They must have thought it was just a tourist bauble she picked up at the myriad of shops in Luxor, but she could tell from experience it was an antique piece, centuries old, that most likely had come from Namire's tomb. But how did it get in her suitcase? She didn't remember cataloging such an item or even seeing such an artifact, yet, here it was. She could be accused of theft, her reputation ruined. She'd be fired if it was discovered she had it. It would be suspicious at the very least. Had Bas put it in her bag as a sick joke? Had Ahmad? Or even Paulette, just to discredit her and her find? If such a scandal came to light, the Egyptian Ministry of Antiquities could demand the immediate return of everything from the tomb and all her work would be for naught.

She wasn't sure what to do as she stared at the statue in her hand. She must've jumped three feet high when another knock came on her door. She quickly put the statue back in her bag, trying to hide it as the door opened and the conductor came in for her ticket. She handed it to him, unable to keep her hand from shaking. She was glad he said nothing about it as he took her ticket and wished her a pleasant day, closing the door once he had departed the room.

She stood and closed the curtain over the door after she locked it. She also closed the window drapes and turned on the light. Once she felt secure enough, she opened the bag and removed the statue for closer examination. If she called it in now, it might appear as if she'd planned on taking it and changed her mind. If she didn't, it'd look like she'd intended to steal the statue all along. The odd thing was, the more she looked over the piece, the more unusual the whole thing was. It was definitely an antique, but far older than Namire's tomb by at least a couple of thousand years, and yet, the statue was in pristine condition. It almost looked like it would come to life any moment. It was reminiscent of Anubis, and yet, that also was different. Would the age be the quantifying factor in the discrepancies?

Carefully, she turned it upside down. There were no engravings, no cartouches, nothing to indicate who it might represent, but Anubis was the only jackal-headed god, so it had to be him or a form of him. Still, the age perturbed her, as well as how it got in her bag. A mystery, to be sure, and one she was not pleased to be involved in, even if she did admire the piece overall.

She set it against the cushions to protect it from the jostling train while she retrieved her briefcase and notes. She needed to record everything she could about it so when she got to Chicago she could notify the Ministry of the additional find, and mention that it was missed in their rush to get everything documented. That should soothe the museum and keep everyone's careers intact.

She had her head buried in her case, and when she looked up again, she screamed, throwing the papers and everything else in her hands into the air. Sitting on the cushions was a life-sized, living, breathing animal. The jackal looked wild and imposing, but it didn't move, watching her with an intense gaze. She didn't know if she should move or not. Hell, she wasn't sure if she was even awake, or if this was just some residual hallucination from the valium she took so she could get on the damned airplane in Egypt.

She hadn't even realized she was moving backward until she hit the wall with nowhere else to go. "Nice jackal." She used a soothing, albeit somewhat shaky voice as she looked around somewhat frantically, realizing there was no escape without going past the animal. Then she looked back at him, puzzled. "Where did you come from? This is a moving train and my door is locked. Oh, shit. I'm going crazy, right? After all, I'm in a locked room, talking to a deadly beast who just appeared out of nowhere. Maybe I'm dead and you're actually Anubis here to lead me into the underworld for judgment. I've flipped. I've actually gone and done what Bas predicted and flipped my frigging lid."

She scrubbed her face, hoping she would wake up from the strangeness of this nightmare.

"You know Bas?"

The rich, accented voice startled her. She screamed again. Looking up, a gorgeous man stood in front of her, half naked. A rich lapis collar with an amulet in the center was around his neck. It was similar to the one she'd seen adorning the statue. Her knees became weak and weren't willing to support her any longer. Moving swiftly, he caught her and moved her slightly to the chair nearby.

"I've gone crazy, right? You were a statue, an animal, and now you're a man who appeared in a locked room on a moving train? And to top it all off, you speak English, even with an accent? Did I die and this is my hell?"

The man pulled back as if offended. "I learned your language a long time ago, as well as many others. That happens when you're as old as I am. I've been called a lot of things in my life, but never someone's hell."

The blood rushed to her cheeks at his admonishment. "I didn't mean it that way." Then caught herself. "Wait. This is my imagination—why am I apologizing?"

"I'm not imaginary. Nor is this a dream. You're alive. At least for the moment."

"For the moment? What does that mean?"

"It means, I need what you've stolen. Give it back now, and I'll let you live."

"I didn't steal the statue! I didn't even know it was in my bag! Besides, I was in the process of reporting it when you showed up."

He gave her an odd look, as if she wasn't making any sense. Then he realized she was referring to him and his statuesque image. He leaned over her imposingly, a snarl on his lips, a growl rumbling against his chest. "Don't play the fool with me. I'm not talking about the statue of me. I'm referring to the box you stole."

She pressed back in her chair as he leaned closer. He was tall and muscular, his biceps looked like pythons, and his hairless bare chest was tanned and ripped. His accent informed her he was Egyptian, and his regal stance implied a form of nobility.

"I don't understand you. Everything we've removed from the temple has been recorded, and the Ministry is aware of what we're taking back with us to the museum. Each item has been appropriately cataloged for shipment."

"Where is it, then?"

"Where is what?" Did he think her a fool and she would just give up the location of precious treasures in her care, even *if* she knew what the hell he was referring to?

"Don't try me, woman. I've little patience for deceit. You know not what you've done by taking it."

"I don't even know what you think I've taken."

"The box. An ornate box from Namire's tomb."

"You're aware of whose tomb—?" She stopped herself before even completing the sentence. How did he know so much?

"Yes. I know it was Namire's resting place, and that you discovered the entrance and proceeded to remove everything from it. Is it on this contraption? Take me to it! Return it at once! It's not yours. You've no idea what you've set in motion."

"You're right. I've no clue what the fudgesicles you're talking about." She couldn't help but notice the slight intonation of reverence whenever he uttered Namire's name. He had mentioned he was old and a brief, ridiculous thought fluttered through her mind...had he known Namire personally? She dismissed the notion almost immediately. That would've been impossible. Yet, then again, so was him being in her locked room.

He growled again, totally impatient this time and slamming his fist on the seat of the chair. "Do I look like an imbecile? By taking it, you've put all of humanity at risk." His head lifted and turned toward the door in concerned surprise. "They're here. Give it to me and you might live through this after all."

"Who's here? Who's going to kill me? I don't know what you're talking about or what you're looking for. I really can't help you."

A knock on the door caused them both to stop arguing and look toward the covered and locked entryway.

"Lyra? I've got your wine."

Asim stood, grabbing her forearm in a tight grip and pulling her up from the chair and away from the door. His closeness made her gasp softly.

"It's my friend." Lyra struggled slightly, fearful of such an imposing man. She had to admit, even in her fear, he was as gorgeous as Bas, but in a darker way.

Bas knocked again. "Come on, Lyra. Open the door. Did you fall asleep?"

She had stopped struggling when she heard Bas. "Help! Help me!" she cried out, resuming her attempts to break free from the stranger's vise-like grip on her arm.

He should've hit her to quiet her down, but he wasn't one to hit a woman just because she was a bit crazy or obstinate. Instead, he covered her mouth with his own. Surprised, she stopped struggling as soon as their lips met.

The door rattled as Bas attempted to gain access.

"We need to go," Asim declared as he pulled back from her. "Please don't scream again. I'm trying to help you."

"But he's my friend. My coworker. He isn't going to harm me. Besides, there's no way out other than the door. In case you haven't noticed, there isn't a whole lot of room on these trains."

Lyra's head spun as Bas knocked again, concern in his voice. "Lyra. Open this instant or I'll break the damned door down. If someone is in there, know I have a weapon and am not afraid to use it."

Weighing the situation, Asim reluctantly nodded toward the door, indicating for her to let Bas enter. Unlocking the door, she stepped aside. He didn't have a weapon, but he had put the wine glasses on the floor and was ready for hand to hand combat if need be. He was a bit surprised when Lyra opened the door, seemingly unharmed.

"Lyra? What's going on?"

She grabbed him and pulled him inside, then reached down for the wine. Tipping one back, she downed the whole thing before she shut the door. Once Bas moved further into the room, he came across the half-naked man staring at him. Turning, Bas looked at her, a scowl on his face. "Who the fuck's this? And what's he doing here? Look, if you were screaming in passion, you should've let me know. I don't go in for that stuff, not even for you."

"Don't be gross, Bas. I have no idea who he is or how he got in here. He just appeared, and he won't leave."

Before she could say anything more, Bas took two steps and was about to slug the man, but Asim's hand caught the flying fist and held fast. Asim was taller than Bas by only a couple of inches, but the strength and power of Asim was far superior. Within a moment, Bas cried out and was on his knees, trying to remove his hand from such a tight clutch.

"Stop. Don't hurt him," she pleaded and Asim gave her a glance that hid his thoughts, although he swiftly complied with her request.

She ran to Bas' side and helped him sit on the couch.

"What's wrong with you? Who are you? What do you want? Can't you just leave us alone?" Lyra was becoming irritated, frantic, and fearful as she snarled at the intruder. She was past caring what he might do as a result of her not cooperating.

"We don't have time for explanations now. It's important that I get the box. Give it to me and you'll never have to see me again."

"Stop. Okay? Just stop. What the hell is going on? I think I deserve some sort of an explanation." Lyra couldn't believe how calm she was being about the whole thing. Albeit a part of her was sure it was just some strange dream and she'd soon wake up with a stiff neck from sleeping on the couch in her stateroom in some odd position.

"What part of we don't have time for explanations now are you not comprehending?" Asim queried, using his height to its fullest, imposing potential.

"None. However, I'm not helping you until I know what's going on, who's after us, and why. Regardless of what you might believe, this train doesn't stop and let people on and off at random, so until it reaches its next scheduled destination, you have time to answer my questions." She backed away from him, returning her attention to Bas' hand.

Bas looked back and forth between them before he spoke up. "Can someone tell me what the fuck is going on? Who is this?" he asked Lyra, but immediately turned to the strange man. "Who the hell are you?"

"Why are you so stubborn? I'm trying to help you stay alive. Just tell me where it is!"

"It's my dream. I can be as obstinate as I please. This can't be real. I don't believe all the things you've done can be real."

Asim wondered how much he should reveal. Although he'd been watching her since the truck pulled away from the dig in Egypt, he realized in the last few minutes she was probably innocent of his accusations. He also really hadn't noticed until now how beautiful she was. Her hair was pulled back, and hints of red could be seen in the dark brown hues of her long strands. Her almond-shaped eyes reminded him of Namire. She had that quiet beauty Namire had, the same shape of her face, the same spirit in her eyes. He turned away, for the thought of Namire, even thousands of years later, still saddened him, and he again wondered what life would've been like had he been able to have her by his side.

While he had taken the moment to gaze upon her before turning away, she had a similar chance to appraise him. His hair was dark, but his eyes were an unusual hue of amber. He had an intense gaze that seemed to penetrate her very soul. Her eyes traveled to his lips and she couldn't help remembering the feel of his kiss against her mouth. She was not naïve enough to believe it anything other than a mechanism just to shut her up, but it was the first time in far too long that she'd been kissed with even a hint of passion. And this man was full of passion and so much assurance. His shoulders were broad, his muscles well toned. He was the poster child for having sculpted abs. He had a chiseled jaw and, if she looked closely, she'd swear she could see a bit of the angular features of the jackal statue in his countenance. She hadn't realized she had been staring until he cleared his throat.

"Tell me where the box is."

"Why?"

"Because it's not yours and you can't keep it."

"Is that what they're after, too? Whoever 'they' are? For that matter, I don't even know who or what you are."

"Yes. They took it and I'd just tracked it down to being hidden in Namire's tomb, but by the time I arrived, it was gone again."

"Okay. Enough with the riddles. Who are they? None of this makes sense, and I'm tired of being in the dark."

"Me, too," Bas spoke up after having watched the exchange between the two of them. "Someone tell me something!"

"My name is Asim. I am second to Anubis. As you've probably guessed, I was the statue you carried until the time was right. 'They' are worshippers of chaos, and they're desperately trying to let evil rule. Do you know of Ma'at?"

Bas and Lyra glanced at each other. Bas looked at her like, *What the fuck is going on?* Lyra just shrugged her shoulders, unsure how to take any of this.

She should be freaking out. After all, the stud

in front of her just told her he was second to a god, and he himself had been a statue she'd held but minutes ago. She didn't believe in magic, and yet, she was taking all the current events as if it were an everyday happenstance.

Lyra nodded in response to his question. "We're archaeologists. I'm Lyra and this is Bas. I'm aware of all the gods. I'm even aware of you, sort of. I've seen depictions of a commander to Anubis' armies, his right-hand man. Ma'at is the goddess of good and justice. It's her feather that is used against the heart when being weighed on the scales in front of Osiris, who presides over the proceedings. These are all myths and legends. Are you trying to tell me they're true? That you are, in fact, centuries old?"

Bas scoffed. "Really, dude? I've heard some tales in my life, but I admit this one is pretty fucking out there."

"Every myth, every legend has to start somewhere; stories told and passed down through the ages. What you've heard about them is all true, well, for the most part. I'd not have appeared to you at all until I was sure where the artifact was, but you called upon Bas and I assumed it was the goddess with whom you were affiliated with. I hadn't expected a male to have the name of a goddess."

"It's short for Sebastian," Bas grumbled.

"Impossible. You'd be tens of thousands of years old." Lyra peered over at Bas to see if he was believing any of this.

Asim nodded. "That's about right."

"And the worshippers of chaos—are they the followers of Set or Apep? Both?" Bas asked, far more calmly than Lyra expected. He was still nursing his hand and watching Asim warily.

Asim inclined his head. "Then you do know. Set, Apep, or any of their followers stole Ma'at's feather, and there's but a limited amount of time in order to get it back to her. If I don't manage within the time limit, or it's damaged before I can return it to her, then good will die and chaos will rule. Set will be king of the land, and all hell will literally break loose into this plane of existence. Now will you tell me? Where is it?"

"The only box I am aware of is the ornate one we found in Namire's sarcophagus. We didn't get a chance to open the box onsite, but we planned on doing so once we got to the museum, after we took the proper precautions. Why did you hide it in her sarcophagus? Or did you forget that was where you put it? Is that how come it took you thousands of years to realize it was in her tomb?"

"I didn't put it there. When Namire was entombed, it hadn't been plundered from Ma'at's temple yet. It was only stolen five days ago, and whoever took it put it in there to give humans access to obtaining it."

"Odd choice," Bas mumbled, settling his injured hand on his lap, though he kept rubbing it. When both looked at him questioningly, he added, "I mean to pick a tomb that we were working on and hadn't even found or opened yet. How did they know we were going to uncover it? How did they get in if it was taken just a few days ago? Why did they choose her tomb to hide it in? After all, what if we hadn't discovered the tomb at all or found the piece? If whoever stole it from Ma'at, surely they would've had access to getting it to a better and more convenient hiding space?"

"They probably figured it would remain undisturbed until Set or his followers were ready to use it. Because they were able to access Ma'at's hiding place, they would've also had the ability to enter the tomb and place it in the sarcophagus, just as they would've known you would find Namire's tomb in time to get it to those who could make the most use out of its powers. I know it was probably one of the gods who took it and placed it for you to find, but Set would've not been personally involved. He is too clever to be caught being so deceptive. Someone else stole it and is assisting him. Apep would've had the most to gain, and as god of darkness he could access it as well. This theft was well planned and executed. A simple thing of it being found by you wouldn't have been an issue, just a means to an end. Now, it's your turn. What museum are you referring to? Where is it located?"

"Chicago. Where this train is heading. The Field Museum. They have the right equipment to carbon date and examine the relics without damage."

"When will we arrive?"

"Tomorrow. The train is due into the city by late morning."

"We can't wait that long. If the followers of Chaos figure it out, and most likely did, they will be after it as soon as possible. It's why they put it there to begin with: so it could be found and put into the hands of fools with little or no clue the power it wields. They most likely realized you would take it there and they could retrieve it easily from that point. If they get there before I do, it'll be the end of life as we know it."

"I can't make the train go any faster than it is, and even if I could, it wouldn't make much of a difference. The items are currently in customs and won't get to the museum for at least another day, either."

"Customs?"

"Yes. It's the federal government's way of making sure the stuff that comes into our country hasn't been stolen or is a threat in any way," Bas spoke up. He oversaw the preparation of items for transport and would be the first one held accountable should something go missing or was recorded improperly.

"And if it is?" Asim relaxed his arms slightly. The more he talked to the two of them, the more he realized they were just pawns in this dire game. Having not been out of Egypt for eons, their assistance could prove valuable, and more time with Lyra was a bonus.

"Then the owners and the people who shipped it are contacted with what the issue is and the result of their findings. Usually, it's just confirmation, maybe a fee, but for this kind of thing, not much happens. It just has to go through the governmental red tape."

"There is no way to get it sooner?"

"Not that I'm aware of. Once it clears customs, then it'll be shipped to the Field Museum." Lyra was starting to relax a bit. At least this was a bit more of the normalcy she was used to. Well, as much as a half-naked Egyptian man who started out as a statue, then turned into a live animal, could be considered normal.

Asim was upset by the news. Bas sat back and crossed his leg over his knee. "There isn't anything to be done until the shipment arrives at the museum. Even then, I'm not sure we can just hand it over. There's a ton of paperwork to be dealt with. The Egyptian Ministry will want every piece accounted for and so will the museum."

"Actually, Bas, we never really got that particular piece fully checked in. We were going to do it when we got to the museum and examined it. I was going to make a preliminary report while we were on the train. Since we don't know what's in the box, no one would know if we found it empty or not." She turned to Asim. "Or, do you need the entire box, too?"

"No. Just the feather from within. Ma'at will have an appropriate containment vessel when it's found and returned to her."

Bas leaned over, uncrossing his legs and lowered his voice to speak to Lyra alone. "Can you really trust him? His story's flipping wacky. You just can't turn over a major piece like that to some loony from the psycho ward."

Lyra gave an apologetic smile to Asim before turning to Bas, her voice also lowered as she leaned in. "I saw it with my own eyes. If this isn't a dream as you both claim, then I've seen things that shouldn't be possible."

She pulled back, and when they both turned to face Asim, he was sitting in the corner, right where he was but a moment ago, only as a jackal. Bas literally jumped up and stood on the couch, as if the height would keep him from the deadly fangs of the animal should it decide to attack.

Lyra, however, didn't react to the change in his physical shape. She surprised herself in her casual response. Noticing Bas' reaction only confirmed to her that what she was seeing was real. She turned back to the jackal. "Look, we'll help you as best we can. If this artifact's as important as you say, then it should be with the rightful owner, but you're going to have to wait until the piece arrives and is released to the museum. Since we never catalogued the interior, it won't be missed. However, talking to you as a dog isn't the easiest thing to do. Nor is having you parade around in public as mostly naked. Bas? Maybe you got something that will fit him? As a man, I mean."

Bas gave her an incredulous look. "My clothes?"

"He won't fit in mine and we can't have him as a jackal. The authorities would have us arrested for transporting a dangerous animal, and he'd be put in a zoo. He certainly can't walk about with the garb he's wearing. It's next to nothing and he'd be arrested for indecent exposure. There's no other choice."

"Sure there is. We call the conductor and say he is a stowaway, forced himself into your cabin, and have him arrested at the next stop or let the zoo have him. Either way is good with me."

She turned to face Bas, a scowl on her face. "Do you really think that's going to work? He has changed from a statue to an animal into a man at will. I highly doubt he'll let you treat him so callously by having him arrested." She took a step closer to him. "Look. We may not have taken the object in question, but it's not ours, either. If he's actually here on behalf of Ma'at and it belongs to her, then all we can really do is help him attain it. Especially if all the good in the world is at stake."

"I don't like the world that much," Bas grumbled. "Fine. Come on, Asim, let's find you some clothes. But if you pee on anything, I'll whop your nose with a rolled-up newspaper."

She couldn't believe how he was talking to Asim. He led the way and the jackal looked at her questioningly.

"Go with him. He's right next door and you need to be better prepared in order to access the museum."

One moment she was talking to the animal, and in the next blink of an eye, the man was once again standing before her. "If he tries to hit me with a newspaper, I'll bite him."

"Fair enough," she smirked, the right side of her lips quirking upward.

"Hey!" Bas exclaimed, folding his arms across his chest.

"You started it by talking about him as if he weren't even in the room," she retorted.

"Fine. Let's go." Bas was already headed to the door and about to grab his glass of wine, but she snatched it before he could.

"I need this more than you right now," she murmured, still trying to wrap her head about the whole, chaotically crazy situation.

Chapter 4

The three of them met up for dinner in the dining car. Asim wore a pair of jeans and a t-shirt that proclaimed, "No is the word of the day." The clothes were a bit tight on him, but it only emphasized Asim and make him more attractive as the shirt pulled across his broad chest and strained to fit around his bulging biceps. Although Bas was built, he was not the hulking behemoth Asim was. Bas whispered to her as they were walking to the diner that he didn't want the clothes back because now they'd be all stretched out and she owed him a replacement for one of his favorite t-shirts. She couldn't help pondering why Bas seemed so out of sorts about Asim and wondered if he were still seething over his hand being crushed. Maybe he felt his ego was bruised as a result, but since no one other than her saw the exchange, she couldn't believe that was the cause. Still, she had no other explanation.

Although Lyra's and Sebastian's meals were included with their tickets, Lyra would foot the bill for their guest. Personally, she felt it was worth the cost of whatever he ate to have the opportunity to discuss everything with him. He had, after all, actually lived in the eras she had always been fascinated with since she was a little girl. Asim provided Lyra the ability to get first-hand accounts of what life was like back then. The three of them talked leisurely about everyday life in the time of the Pharaohs for hours, going through two bottles of wine in the process. The dining steward eventually prodded them to head back to their rooms, as he was shutting the car down for the night.

As they walked back to Lyra's room, Bas decided he was too tired to remain with them and begged off at his own cabin door. "I had the steward set up the other bed for you, Asim." He slid the door open, waiting for the tall Egyptian to enter first.

"You're welcome to come to my room if you wish to finish our conversation. I really am interested in knowing first-hand about the religious ceremonies at the various festivals."

Asim nodded. "I'll be honored to continue our discussion."

"Fine. If you need me, Lyra, just pound on the wall or something." Although his words were addressed to her, he gazed unerringly at Asim, as if in warning that he would come to her aid should she require it. Despite the slight injury to his hand earlier, he wouldn't be deterred from protecting her. Asim smirked but said nothing. He was well aware of what Bas was trying to do with his veiled threat and it didn't bother him in the least.

In truth, Asim enjoyed talking to Lyra. She was intelligent and inquisitive. Plus, it didn't hurt that she was enjoyable to gaze upon. Given the choice between sleeping with another male in the room or having the company of a beautiful woman, he would choose the woman any day. It was extremely rare, no, actually, he couldn't even remember a time when a woman wanted to be with him. Truth be told, after Namire, he pretty much had very little interest in any woman, until Lyra.

Lyra stepped towards Bas, resting her hand lightly on his arm in hopes of reassuring him. "I promise to pound repeatedly and scream if I need you." She realized the conversations over dinner and wine emboldened her, making her less fearful of Asim with each passing moment and instead left her fascinated. She moved past Bas' room, returning to her own accommodations, ushering Asim inside so as not to disturb Bas.

She hoped once the two of them were alone she could steer the conversation towards Namire. Was it her imagination or did Asim seem to shy away from anything to do with Namire during their dinner? He admitted he knew her briefly, and he was saddened by her death. He mentioned Namire had been murdered, but refused to discuss anything more. Hopefully in the privacy of her cabin he'd be more open to discussing the daughter of Horemheb. Of course, another bottle of wine wouldn't hurt, either, and she'd brought one back from the dining car with her.

Once inside, she shut the door. Her bed had already been pulled down, but there was a chair he could sit on while she sat opposite him on the bed. She figured the wine needed to be consumed before she gained the additional courage to steer the conversation back towards Namire. They spent a little time discussing the festivals, then she turned the conversation to him and his curious abilities.

Asim was getting caught up in the conversation. No one ever asked him how he came to be. With the passage of time, few even knew he was once a human, or that Anubis converted him to serve as his second. He found himself very vocal about how he became Anubis' commander and why he needed to be changed in order to lead Anubis' army on his behalf into battle all those eons ago. As he regaled her with stories of the gods and how Anubis turned him, she realized Asim was the start of the werewolf legends. Jackals were similar to wolves. As years progressed and stories retold, it was not surprising things would somewhat change; like kids sitting in a circle playing telephone. When the story had been told a few times, it was different from how it began.

Their consumption of wine encouraged her to finally ask again about Namire. Maybe with the wine and relaxed company, he'd share what she really desired to know.

"You said you knew Namire. I always suspected Horemheb had a daughter. I figured if he had a son, his name would've been all over the place as the next in line. Horemheb's tomb had been discovered over a hundred years ago, yet no one ever found Namire's tomb. It was certainly well hidden. Are there others that are hidden that well?" *That's it, Lyra. Ease in from another angle and maybe he won't notice and give up more information.*

"No."

She blinked at him, then reached over and gave his thigh a slap laughing. "Gee, don't be so descriptive."

Asim shifted uncomfortably in his seat. Suddenly those memories of Namire that had been resurfacing since he had visited her tomb came pouring forth in a flash flood he was unable to stop. Although the wine shouldn't have affect him like humans, he found himself talking about her.

"Namire." He said her name with a reverence he hadn't spoken with, even when he was discussing Anubis and the other gods. She remained quiet, seeming to know he needed to tell the story in his own way. Instinctively, she knew there was more to Namire than just an acquaintance for him.

"Namire was more than just Horemheb's daughter. She was his only heir and should've been queen upon his death. By then, however, her mother had long since passed away and her step-mother refused to acknowledge her very existence. Namire didn't care though. She was fine as long as she had a roof over her head and didn't starve. She hated the limelight and willingly stood back from her father and his second wife, Mutnedjmet."

"How did she die? I know our examination of her will tell me her story, but it won't be as personal as you're telling me. How did you even know her? Meet her? What did she look like? What did she think about things? Was she helpful or did her staying in the background keep her distant from the everyday people?" So much for taking it slowly.

"Whoa. So many questions so quickly. First, I met her when she came to Anubis' Temple to ask for mercy on Horemheb's trial. She was sure his heart would be heavy from all the decisions he made for the Egyptian people. She was beautiful, but it was more than just physical beauty. Her ka was gentle and kind, loving. She stayed in the background in hopes of aiding those who needed her assistance, even though as a woman she couldn't do much. She did have the ear of her father, though, and when she saw something he could remedy, she would beseech him to fix it. I didn't know her well, but we were to be married. I was just starting to get to know her when she was murdered."

"You were engaged? I thought you didn't know her well. Why would you marry someone you didn't know? Was it arranged?"

"No. Not arranged like you mean. We had briefly met, and I didn't know much about her when I asked her to move in with me. In those days, getting married was when a couple simply moved in together and signed a marriage contract. There were no complicated ceremonies or rituals needed. It was very uncomplicated and a mutual resolution between the two parties. As for why? That's hard to explain. Anubis once told me my jackal-self would know when they met the one they were interested in. One who would understand who and what I was and be accepting of it. They would love me unconditionally and I would feel that bond between us before I was even aware of it. That was how I felt with Namire. Something about her called to me, to my jackal. I could feel him twitching beneath my skin wanting her, desiring to make her mine. She must have felt the same, for she seemed drawn to me as much as I was to her. It was only after her death and the deaths of her killers that I learned how truly kind and unselfish she was. She would've been my perfect mate had we been given the full chance to be together."

"I'm sorry. She sounds incredible. I understand why it's so hard for you to talk about. You must miss her terribly, even after all this time. I can tell by the way you speak of her. You said she was murdered! Who would dare kill the daughter of a Pharaoh? That would be like killing a god, wouldn't it?"

"Thank you. I do miss her. I hate that the pettiness of the time resulted in her demise and we were never really given a chance. As for being murdered? Yes, in a way it's true. It would be the same punishment as killing a living god. However, there is a dispensation when one is prompted by another living goddess. In this particular case, Mutnedjmet instigated the deed. She incited the crowd to stone Namire for crimes against her newly deceased father. It was Mutnedjmet's way of securing her place on the throne since she had been unable to bear the king an heir. When I learned of her death..." Asim paused, his jaw clenching as he tried to regain control of his emotions and wondered why he was telling Lyra all of this. She gazed at him, waiting patiently, her deep, dark eyes peering at him with a kindness he'd only seen once before. "When I learned of her death, I found her body tossed aside as if she were garbage, and it incited rage from deep within that I can't even try to put into words. Her body was beaten and battered almost beyond recognition. Mutnedjmet threw the first stone and encouraged others to do the same. Once the villagers' frenzy had been incited, they stoned her. When no other stones could be found, they kicked her and beat her with sticks or other tools. Even after she was long dead, they continued to wage war against her body.

I found what was left of her mutilated remains and I brought her to the tomb of her father. I told the priests of Anubis to bury her in a side chamber originally started for Mutnedjmet, and to quickly establish another for Horemheb's wife. I used my powers to abolish Mutnedjmet's name from the room and put in Namire's cartouche. I got the sarcophagus and had her embalmed. While the embalming process was being dealt with, I gathered a stone carver to put the Book of the Dead in her tomb. There wasn't much time for anything else. I then sealed it, so none would be the wiser she was buried with her father. In the meantime, Mutnedjmet erased even the minimal aspects of her very existence, wiping Namire from history. But Mutnedjmet couldn't erase her from my memory. I've kept her alive in my mind and heart all these centuries." Asim didn't add that, while the priests were busy with his instructions and the embalmers were handling the preparation of the body, he returned to the palace and attacked everyone who had even a hint of Namire's scent on them. He made it his personal mission to make each and every bastard involved suffer a death of their very own at his hands, saving Mutnedjmet for last. By the time he got to the queen, she was quaking in her golden slippers. He made sure she knew she had brought this upon herself and she would be made to suffer the most. He dragged her to a private embalming chamber and had them start the embalming process while the queen was still alive.

He was so infuriated and disheartened over Namire's loss he had little care of the consequences of his actions. If anything, maybe he was forfeiting his own life in the process, but that only meant he would meet Namire in the afterlife that much sooner. Anubis vouched for him, though, and let him grieve in his own way, even if that meant the deaths of dozens.

Asim poured the last of the wine into Lyra's cup and tossed the empty bottle. Standing, he looked down at her. Gods, she reminded him of Namire, and his whole body tingled at remembering their one and only time together. He'd never felt the same since Namire, at least, until now. He wanted Lyra with the same intensity as he had Namire all those centuries ago. A brief thought entered his mind. Was it his animal wanting to claim her as he had Namire all those centuries ago? Or was it his imagination because Lyra reminded him of Namire? Like his princess, Lyra had a quiet gentleness to her, almost a sadness that she used to keep the world at bay and not let any get too close to her. He wasn't sure of her story and would have to ask her later on about it, but he was too emotionally wrought now to give her the attention her story would definitely need from him. For the moment, it was enough she was interested in his musings of the one and only woman who had ever touched his life so profoundly.

"I should go."

Lyra stood with him. "Sure. You must be tired."

"Not really. I don't require as much sleep as

most do. Battle trained and ready."

"Makes sense after what you told me. However, do you still find yourself being called into battle?" Her hand absentmindedly went to her lips. No matter what they talked about or how hard she tried, the thought of his lips on hers was always on her mind.

"No. The battles I deal with are more internal. I still have my duties for Anubis while he is leading others to their trials, but even that doesn't keep me busy of late. None worship the gods of old as they had eons ago. Men make their own war and call on foreign gods to guide them. There is little left for me to do." When he saw her rise, he added, "I don't need you to escort me to Bas' quarters. I remember the way."

Lyra laughed. "That's not what I was doing." Maybe she had a bit too much wine, or maybe his story touched some deep part of her that she couldn't quite let go, or maybe the thought of that kiss was just a bit too much for her to get over. Either way, she didn't care. She stepped up to him and pulled his head down to kiss him.

Asim was surprised by her actions. Modern women confounded him, and this one even more so. He wanted to grab her and deepen the kiss, but thoughts of Namire, of taking her so rashly and the resulting dire outcome, caused him to push her back.

Lyra's face fell. "Am I too bold for you? Are you not interested?"

"Interested? Hell, yes, I'm interested. We just met, though, and you've had a number of surprises today. Besides, what about Sebastian?"

She reached up to cup his cheek with her hand. "Bas is a friend. A good, dear friend, but nothing more. I know we just met, but I feel that this opportunity won't happen again. I want this to happen."

"Are all modern women this brazen?"

Her eyes became hooded; she didn't remove her palm and instead moved in closer, a hairs-breadth from his lips. "Sometimes. Personally? I usually go after what I want, but I'm sure the wine has given me extra courage. I don't think I want to wait."

His brow furrowed slightly in confusion as he tipped her features back with a thumb. "Wait?"

Her cheeks flushed with wine; she smiled softly. She almost wanted to laugh at the way the two of them danced around each other, and yet she sensed they both wanted more. "As in, I want this."

His blood began to pound within his veins, mouth drying as he fought to find words to say something. Anything. His jackal sprung to life, twitching to be free and claim her.

His hesitation made her frown slightly and she backed up. Guess he didn't want her after all. Her voice was soft as a whisper on the wind. "It's okay. I'm sorry I misread your attention. I should've realized after the way you talked about Namire that I wouldn't be of interest to you."

Throwing his common sense to the wind, Asim threw his arms around Lyra, pulling her flush against him. "I need you more than you could ever know. I didn't want to scare you with how much I desire you. My hesitation and silence had nothing to do with Namire or how I feel about her. I find you as interesting as her when I first met her. It's a feeling I hadn't felt since she crossed into the afterlife. I just want you to be sure this is what you want and not some fantasy, because I am what you're archeologically interested in brought to life." His arms tightened around her.

She was slightly startled at his reaction, especially after he'd seemed so hesitant just a moment ago. His hard body pressed against her, those steel arms wrapped around her, and her breathing stopped momentarily. His ear near her mouth, her warm breath tantalizing his skin, she whispered softly, "I have no illusions to who or what you are. This isn't some private fantasy being fulfilled. I want it all. I want you for you."

Moving his head, his lips captured hers. Fingers moved to cup her head as he heard the magic words to keep going. He couldn't stop, not anymore. Not if he wanted to. But he had learned his lesson. He'd go slowly, treat her with respect, not the rush job he did with Namire, just in case this was their only intimate moment. He'd take his time and show her just how much he wanted her. He couldn't be close enough, couldn't get enough of her sweet taste. His tongue slipped inside her mouth, sweeping along her warmth before tangling with hers.

Lyra moaned softly as chills ran up and down her spine.

He growled, "Bloody hell. You're amazing!"

"It does get better, if memory serves me right. I mean, I know it's been a while for me, but I think I remember how it's done and I don't think that was it." She chuckled softly against his skin. Licking his neck from his collarbone to his ear, she swirled her tongue around its curves before sucking his earlobe into her mouth.

He growled low as her tongue played with his sensitive spots. Gods, he had to keep his control so as not to just force her down and take her. His jackal was snarling at the hold Asim had on him. He wanted free to claim her, to take her for himself. He wanted to bite her and make her his for eternity, but Asim wouldn't allow the jackal to be that free. He wouldn't hurt Lyra, wouldn't force anything from her that she didn't offer to give freely herself. But, dear gods, it was hard to keep his jackal part held back.

"Are you sure about this?"

"Mmhmm."

"Are you a virgin?"

She snorted. "No."

How could he even think with the way she used her lips? "I haven't felt this way in quite some time. If you want to stop, now's the time. What would make you happiest?"

"You not asking so many questions about what would make me happiest."

He snarled, tugging her head gently with both hands as he crushed their lips against each other. "No more questions."

Melting against him, she dared not move or shift position, not that she could anyway; he held her so tightly.

Asim pulled his lips from Lyra's to gently kiss

and nip the smooth column of her neck. She tilted her head back to give him better access to her throat, her silken hair caressed his arms as they wrapped about her.

Asim shifted slightly. No going back. He wanted to take things slow, but feeling her so close was challenging. Her very essence and taste drove him to the brink of insanity.

Pushing back from him slightly, she pulled out his shirt from his pants, letting her hands slip over his skin while she tugged it over his head. She nuzzled against the hollow of his throat, taking in the whole of him, feeling her own body respond.

Drawing the fabric of her shirt, Asim mimicked her movements to slip his hand along her stomach, feeling goosebumps raise from his touch.

He pulled her shirt off, tossing it among the discarded clothing piling on the floor.

He brought her as close to him as possible. Flesh against bare flesh. Hands moved to gently grip her hips, his lips pulled from hers to plant kisses to her neck, moving to her breasts. His hands reached up to cup each lacy mound.

She shivered lightly, not from cold, but from the explosion of nerves. This was right. He was right, and it felt so immensely good. She moaned and muttered soft sweet nothings as his lips moved down her body. He pushed her back onto the made-up bed. Her hands still trailed over the skin of his back and arms, feeling his corded muscles bunch under her fingertips. She rolled him over and straddled him, letting him continue to explore her body as she would do to him.

She gazed into his eyes, dark with passion. He had touched a part of her no one had for a long time, if ever. His look told her how much he desired her. Lyra knew her look to him was the same. Her eyes were dark, her breathing shallow with anticipation.

Eagerly, Asim kissed her, their tongues tangling in a dance of pure passion. He could feel the heat between them.

He made sure she was comfortable with how quickly they were moving, even though she'd told him this was what she wanted. He enjoyed her moaning as he felt her nipples harden to peaks under his hand.

The sounds made his already stiff member harden even more. She could feel him throbbing against her inner thigh. She understood his hesitation wasn't a result of not doing anything for him; instead, he was concerned he would scare her away, even though she'd started this. She wanted to let him know she didn't frighten easily. Sitting up, she reached around and undid her bra, slipping it off and hoping it would show him she was not timid. Taking his hand, she put it on her breast again.

He growled, eyes glazing over in lust. He wouldn't lose control, he couldn't! But by the gods, when she freed herself from the damned lace and placed his hand again to her breast, he wanted to lay her down and have her! His lips curled around the nipple freed from its confinement, gently suckling before biting so gently. Had she any clue of what she did to him? She had to. While one hand still cupped a heaving breast, his free hand moved to unzip her jeans.

Lyra thought she was going to come just from his mouth sucking her peaked pebble. He set her blood aflame, every nuance heightened, every touch singeing her. She had never wanted someone this badly. Did he feel it, too? She felt his hand working her jeans and she hoisted herself slightly to let him pull them and her panties off her hips. In turn, she mimicked him, her hands sliding down his body—not wanting to stop touching his skin—to open his pants' closure.

Feeling her move and wriggle caused a moan to escape. Although she pulled away slightly in order to help pull the material off her form, he hated to have her part from his heated body for even a second. Asim grinned as he felt fingers tug his jeans. He decided to let her do this so as not to spoil her fun. He wasn't quite willing to expose all his powers at once.

Once she managed to undo his jeans, she slid a hand inside to rest lightly above the top of his curls. She was bare now, yet it was her eyes he stared at and held.

His breathing increased its rate, eyes half-lidded to feel her fingers resting so close to his throbbing need. He reached forward to brush against her pubic curls, lightly grazing her outer folds in a gentle manner. With his free hand, he gently pressed the heel of her palm down, hissing as he felt her fingers grasp his cock.

He adored her hand on his erection, the way she moaned. Shifting over slightly, she moved his pants off him, releasing him as her hands slid the jeans along his muscular legs. How erect he stood, his tip shimmering with pre-cum. She reached out again and slid her hand over the leaking moisture and down around him. He could smell her juices pooling between her legs with her excitement.

He reciprocated the action, gently moving her to lie on her back, fingers continuing their rhythm against her satiny heat. He felt her juices coat his fingers, making it easier to slip a digit inside her core, growling at how tight she was.

Gasping as he invaded her sex, she arched slightly, wiggling under him. Her hand barely fit around him as she glided up and down the hardened length. The man was big, and it set her own juices on fire. She opened her legs a bit wider for him.

There wasn't a part of his body she didn't want to touch or feel. As her hand slid over him and neared the hilt, she opened her fingers and let her hand rub his balls. This man was intoxicating, and she knew she could become addicted to him.

His tongue licked her lower lip while he slowly pulled his finger out, leaving only the tip against her sex before pressing again inside. Her hand was small in comparison to his own, but as she grasped him, it was the sweetest touch he'd ever known and set his blood to pounding within his veins.

Asim's head tilted back as Lyra cupped his sac, her touch nearly sending him over the edge. With a shake of his head, he leaned down, capturing her lips with his before capturing her hands to keep over her head. He looked down into those bright eyes, ensuring everything was all right before he'd continue. He just needed to see she was still okay.

"Asim? Is everything okay?"

He murmured softly, "I just want to make sure you're ready."

"Yes. I'm ready."

He noticed the impish gleam in her eyes. He released the breath he'd been holding. If she'd said no, he'd have attempted a way to try and convince her otherwise. Resting his forehead to her own, he smiled, slowly pressing his member to her outer folds, waiting for a second before he pushed in, hissing at how tight she was around him, how her channel cuddled his fully hardened cock.

She swallowed, then gasped, moaning as he slid inside her, filling her completely. She couldn't believe how good he felt. She raised her hips as he set the rhythm, feeling him go deeper as she met each of his thrusts with a push of her own. Her head leaned back as shivers coursed through her. She let her hands slide down his back and over his contracting ass cheeks as he plunged in and out of her heated core. She trembled under him slightly, her nerves soaking up every nuance, his warm breath sending more shudders down her spine while the rest of her blood heated up. She brought her legs up, wrapping them around him as he continued to excite her with his rod. She tried to maintain a locked gaze, but there were certain thrusts that just sent her body to ecstasy and she had to close her eyes momentarily and moan or hiss. Could this be any more perfect?

Seeing her spine arch as she writhed and mewled from pleasure brought a proud snarl from him. One large hand wrapped around her leg, the other about her waist as he increased his tempo. Repeatedly, he'd press into her heated core. "Lyra," he groaned, eyes closed as his head snapped back.

She opened her eyes as he called her name and saw pure unadulterated bliss on his face. He said himself it'd been a while for him and she didn't think he would lie to her, but still, it made her smile that she could give this to him. Not that she was complaining on what he was doing to her, 'cause, gods have mercy on her soul, this felt awesome. She panted slightly, moaning softly. "Asim. Oh, yes!"

Asim watched her features twist and contort to pleasure, stroking her tight, hot channel with his member as his hands moved from her trembling form to grip the sheets beneath her. He tried his damned hardest not to rip them to shreds as he felt his resolve slipping. Asim felt himself grow larger, harder, while he continued his titillating torture on her willing body. He pulled her legs from his waist and hoisted them into the air.

This position sent a whole new set of heated chills through her body. She could smell the two of them together, hear the slapping of skin against skin. Her nails dug into his shoulders as she started to build. Her body tightened around him as she met each thrust he made into her. She didn't know how much longer she'd be able to hold back what her body cried out for the most. A light sheen of sweat had built between them from the heat of their bodies. "Just a little more. Please, Asim, don't stop."

He hissed, giving one quick nod to show he understood. No way he'd ever leave her unsatisfied.

She had to join him in that ultimate gratification, and he'd see to it they'd reach it together. Reaching for one of her hands, he intertwined their fingers. "Lyra! Tell me you're close. Tell me you want to come." Asim continued his thrusts, feeling her walls clench his shaft tightly. He could feel she was almost there. He needed her to come first. He had to know he fulfilled her, gave her enjoyment before he took his own. He'd learned from experience. He'd do it right this time. He'd make sure she got satisfaction first.

She could barely breathe. He knew just what to do, where to touch, how to push against her just right so she literally saw stars. He held most of her body suspended off the bed, one hand on the arm he was using to hold her legs up while her other hand clutched his shoulder. The world stood still for one split moment, then shattered into a million shimmering pieces as she softly cried out his name, coming like she never had before.

He released a bestial howl, his fingers gripping her hips so hard bruises were sure to appear later. Feeling Lyra's orgasm milking his member, he couldn't help joining her, feeling his hot seed racing inside her womb. He rested his forehead to her own, gasping and panting for breath. "Gods. That was amazing, Lyra."

She chuckled. "Makes me sound like a circus act." She brushed her fingers in his hair softly, trying to get oxygen back into her burning lungs. "Come see the Amazing Lyra." She chuckled again, her nervousness taking over as she shivered slightly within his arms. "But yes, it was amazing."

He chuckled, unable to stop himself as he rolled to his side, pulling himself out slowly. His fingers moved to caress her cheeks, bringing her to rest against him. "Good. I'm glad I pleased you. Ready for round two?"

Chapter 5

Lyra had spent the last hour on the phone with the museum to check on the shipments and make sure the lab was ready for them upon arrival. They wouldn't open any of the crates until she was there personally, along with the manifest. That would give her and Bas time to figure out where the box with the feather was, so it could be properly returned to its rightful owner. Honestly, she was still surprised she believed everything that happened yesterday. If someone told her just two days ago that she would believe in a mystical world with magical beings she would've laughed her ass off, then given them the name of a good psychiatrist. Yet, here she was accepting a man could be a statue, then a live animal, and finally an unbelievable man who certainly knew his way around pleasing a woman.

Her inner thighs were achy from their activities last night and she couldn't help but smile at the thought of what they did together, nor how often. Being what he was must've explained his prowess and ability to recharge so often and so quickly, unlike a human male. Every time she was sure he was done, he asked her for another round. After the seventh time, she called 'uncle' and today she was paying the price with tender loins and sore, achy muscles. But, damn, it was so worth it. Had she ever felt this way before? Maybe at first with Bas, but it didn't last and that was part of their problem. It wasn't Bas' fault. It wasn't hers, either. It just happened. She loved him, but more like a brother, a shoulder she could lean on, someone she knew would always be there for her, supporting her. But the 'let's have a mind-blowing sexual experience' just didn't quite work and she found she couldn't love him that way. At least, not after her parents died. To be truthful, especially to herself, she knew she changed drastically since 9/11. For a long while, she was in shock and disbelief. Then numb to everything around her. She didn't care about anything. Each day was a drudgery just to find a reason to get out of bed and face the day. It wasn't until Bas pushed her to complete her thesis that she found something to cling onto. Horemheb's daughter. She was sure, positive even, that he had a child, and it stood to reason the child was from his first marriage. She became obsessed with trying to prove a daughter existed, that she wasn't crazy. The paper was more than just an idea, it was a lifeline, and she needed something to pull her out of her depression.

Bas encouraged her, reminded her that her parents would want her to complete her studies. She had to make them proud and not just waste each day of her life because life didn't end for her. She had to continue on, make something of herself, make them proud of her, and she took his words to heart, delving into the project with everything she had to give. Yet, it didn't leave much for him, or anything or anyone else. She lived in the past because there it was safe. Until Asim. Maybe because he lived through the past, she was intrigued with him. Maybe it was something more. She truly felt she could literally go crazy trying to figure it out. She knew she should just accept it as one of the best nights she could remember for a very long time; revel in the memories of his touch against her skin, the feel of him inside of her, the way he brought her body to life instead of her just existing and trying to get through each day. She let in feelings she hadn't permitted herself to indulge in and it was disconcerting, throwing her slightly off balance. She had to force herself to focus on work and retrieving what Asim came for, even though she knew it meant he would then be gone, most likely for good. He'd become part of her past and she wondered if she'd be able to continue to move forward or if she would fall back into the safeness of becoming an emotional recluse once again.

She rubbed her face. She really had to stop thinking so much, but that was also one of her newest issues: the what ifs and maybes, even if they were in the future and not just the past. She knew she should live in the present, but that was the hardest thing for her to do.

Washing up, because taking a shower on a moving train was a feat in and of itself, even though she had a private one in her room and all she had to do was sit on the toilet seat, was still more of an adventure than she cared for. Once clean and dressed, she sent a text to Bas to have him and Asim meet her in the dining car for their morning meal.

During breakfast, she could tell Bas had a restless night as well. Asim was the only one who looked rested and ready for whatever the day might bring.

After their tryst, Asim retired to Bas' room, not

wanting to disgrace her by staying with her the whole night. She thought his chivalry sweet, albeit a long-lost concept that really didn't fit in with today's ideals. Still, she spent the early morning hours just thinking about him, about the feather, and about their conversations. Her mind was awhirl with everything she learned, and she couldn't settle down enough to get any decent rest, even though he'd done his best to make her completely exhausted. Now, though, she was so tired that even coffee didn't help. They discussed plans for when the train pulled into Union Station. From there, they would catch a cab to bring them the couple of miles to the Field Museum. She knew Bas couldn't wait to find the feather and turn it over, though she wondered why he was so anxious about it—almost, dare she say, jealous.

After breakfast they returned to their rooms. During the entire affair, Asim barely glanced at Lyra and she had to wonder about it. Maybe it hadn't meant anything to him after all? She was, admittedly, the one who instigated their tryst, and now it seemed as if it was over before it actually began. At least to him. The slight ache she had thinking about it was a solid reminder of why she hadn't let herself live in the present. The past was hard enough, but at least it was also safer.

Once they arrived in Chicago, she led the two men through the Great Hall and onto the street where they could hail a taxi. Asim spent the first few minutes gazing up at the tall buildings, then the hubbub of people passing by. He kept his nose pressed to the window as the vehicle drove down

Jackson Street to Columbus, to Lake Shore Drive, and to the back of the Field Museum. Bas paid the driver while the three of them got out. Lyra led Asim inside and to the back area where the crates would arrive, if they hadn't already.

The halls twisted and turned, but they saw few others as they walked to the cargo receiving area. She grabbed the manifest just outside the door and saw the shipment had already arrived. "It came in two hours ago. Had the train not been late, we probably would've beaten it. This means they won't be in holding, they would've been processed and brought to my section," she explained to Asim.

She led Asim back through the halls to her work area. It was a large cargo space, made smaller with all the boxes and crates it now contained.

As they entered, she stopped, her mouth agape in shock and dismay. Bas glanced around the room in disbelief while Asim pushed past them both, cautiously stepping over the strewn remnants of the crates. The room was in total shambles. The boxes opened, lids tossed aside, and the items they contained rummaged through. Someone had obviously been looking for something, and the only thing that made sense was that they were also looking for the feather.

"Which box?" Asim growled as he moved debris out of his way, trying to use his senses to find it.

Lyra looked at the numbers as well as the sizes of the crates. After several frustrating minutes, she pointed out where it should be, only the crate was broken and the ornate box containing the feather was gone. Asim howled in utter vexation. He let his arm swish, clearing a table of its contents and spilling them to the floor. He was about to repeat the process when Lyra stepped up and caught his arm. "Please don't break anything else. I know you're upset, but destroying all the other artifacts isn't going to help and you'll ruin other items of importance." At first, she didn't think he was going to comply, but then she added softly, "These are things of Namire's and we shouldn't make her pay with the loss of items that keeps her memory alive."

Her touch made him pause and he stared in disbelief at her. She dared to stop him, even when it could've harmed her for suddenly getting in his way? However, when she mentioned Namire, his anger deflated to acquiesce to her request. It took him a couple more breaths to relent from taking his rage out on the remaining objects.

"These are precious historical pieces that can't be replaced," she emphasized.

He snarled at her, though his tone wasn't as cruel as he wanted it to be. "You don't seem to understand. These items and everything else you know won't be important if good dies. What you'd be left with is chaos and evil. The world won't care about historical artifacts. It'll be too busy trying to survive, and most likely disintegrate into total annihilation."

Bas watched the exchange between them, his eyes narrowing. Lyra was placing herself in harm's way, and if Asim tried anything, Bas would be there in a second, regardless of how badly he might fail. He couldn't believe how relaxed Lyra was, as if she didn't have a care in the world, not even the fate of it. However, he also knew Lyra very well. It was her coping mechanism: to remain calm in the direst of circumstances. Then when she was alone with time to process, she'd break down, releasing all the emotions and fears she'd kept hidden previously. She thought of herself as an emotional recluse, but he knew her too well to believe it. She kept herself numb to feelings to avoid the pain of her loss, but he knew she would lose control when she thought no one else would be the wiser. He continued to let her believe what she needed to for her own sanity.

"I do understand, Asim. But, I'm also aware that if we lose our heads, we won't be able to find it."

"And how do you propose we do that now?" Asim growled, albeit more gently than before, calming with each passing moment.

"We can start with the security tapes to see who's been in here. That might give us a clue where to go to next. I've faith that we'll find it before it's destroyed and all is lost."

Bas spoke up. "I'll head over to the security office and see if we can get them pulled up. I'll notify Michelle of the breach, as well." Bas sent Asim a warning glance to not touch Lyra or anything else while he was gone. When he was sure Asim understood his glare, he headed out of the room without another word.

Lyra was about to follow him, but Asim gently touched her arm to halt her progression. He wasn't sure what it was about her that caused him to respond so easily to her. Was it because, in an odd way, she reminded him of Namire? Her strength, her courage? She did and said what was on her mind, and he found it refreshing. "I'm sorry."

She gave him a blinding smile. "I understand. I really do get the urgency of what you're trying to achieve. You've asked for my assistance and I'm going to do my best to help you."

"Actually, I accused you of stealing it." His lips twitched slightly as he held back a smirk.

"True. You had me at a disadvantage watching me from the site."

His hand reached up, his forefinger caressing her cheek. He stepped closer and she held her breath. She could feel her cheeks flaming in remembrance of the tryst on the train. Was he planning on kissing her again? She hoped so. She wasn't one to give in to impulses, but there was something about him, something that touched her inside, that she had thought didn't exist. After all, Bas tried and she was barely moved for anything other than friendship with him, and he was perfect for any woman. Any woman, that is, except her. So why was she drawn in by Asim? Could the fact he lived an era of history she was so enamored with be what fascinated her enough to lower her guard with him? Or did the idea that the fate of the world was in their hands and, if they failed, so did the world, have anything to do with her interest in him? A 'last chance' kind of thing?

He pulled his hand back and she was immensely disappointed. It left her feeling at odds with herself. She had let herself become too vulnerable and he had barely acknowledged her existence, save for a moment ago, since they were intimate the previous evening. He took what she gave him, gave her a night to remember, enabled her to feel things she hadn't thought possible any longer, but he didn't really care about her other than as a passing fancy. After all, what guy was going to turn down sex? Isn't that what they always think about? Lyra provided the ability for him to have it. She was a vessel for his lust and she gave herself to him with nary a thought. The wine didn't help either. But it was obvious he didn't feel the same way and wouldn't have seduced her if she hadn't thrown herself at him. She cleared her throat and looked anywhere but at him. "Let's see what Bas has found out for us." She turned and left the room, keeping her eyes away from him.

He shouldn't have touched her. She wasn't Namire, and, although there was something about Lyra that called to him, he had yet to figure it out. He needed to keep his head in the game; the stakes were too high to get lost in whatever nonsense he was feeling. He had to force himself to trail after her, grateful she was in front of him so he could shift his cock around slightly to get a bit more comfortable. Just the look in her eyes, the touch of her skin, and he grew hard with a desire for her unlike anything he had felt before or since Namire. And that sense of familiarity threw him each time he got close to her, like he had known her most of his long life. How he wished he could give her more of what they shared last night. He didn't want to leave her even then. He wanted to hold her close in his arms and actually sleep with her warm, naked body against his, then repeat everything when they woke up on the train, letting the swaying car enhance his own thrusting movements. He wanted to scoop her up and over his shoulder and carry her away where he could spend hours upon hours in her company, feasting on her like the hungry man he was. He knew if he gave in, even for just a brief kiss, like he almost did just moments ago, he would succumb to her entirely. Already he was on the brink of being lost totally in her presence and understanding when she was near, he couldn't concentrate on his duty. He needed to focus on his task, so despite the wonderful view of her ass walking away, and the disappointment he felt from her, he silently followed her.

Chapter 6

Four men got out of the truck with their treasure in a satchel. Lanky and tall, Virgil Jones headed to the garage door, closing and securing it. Erik Bond and his brother, David, walked upstairs to the small office and adjoining lounge, flipping on the game console to pick up *Call of Duty* where they had left off before departing the old hangar. They were both big, rotund men with scraggily beards and arm-sleeve tattoos. The difference between them was Erik had long hair and David had a shaved head, which also sported a tattoo of a skull. Chase Green, the most assured-looking, clean-cut man in the group, took the satchel to a room off the garage. He also bore a couple of tattoos on his arms and a prominent tattoo of Set on his chest, as well as Set's symbol on his hand. His dark hair was trimmed short, and if he wore a business suit, he'd pass in business society. He reached for a key on his belt to open the door. The room was one of only a few places he kept under lock and key, but it served to keep the others out of his business. Although Jones and the Bond brothers were good men, they weren't quite as committed to the overall mission as he was, so he kept his secrets from them and told them only what he felt they needed to know. Besides, truth be told, he felt they weren't quite the smartest tools in the chest, as they could only seem to keep up with one step of their operation at a time. Chase knew when the time came, his accomplices, and others within the cult, would be collateral damage to make way for the new world about to exist. Chase, on the other hand, would be one of the leaders, obtaining an elite position within the chaotic world. After all, if not for him, Set wouldn't be released. He was also aware he'd be heavily rewarded as a result of his endeavors.

The room Chase unlocked was dark, the walls painted black. It was windowless but cavernous. Once an old storage space for airplanes, it fit his needs perfectly. Along one wall several brown robes hung from hooks. Along another were instruments for their ceremonies. In the center of the room was an altar surrounded by several pillars holding melted candles, with additional burned-down candles spread about the room. Finally, in the back of the building was a twenty-foot-tall statue of Set with two spotlights illuminating the magnificent sculpture, which Chase turned on when he entered. Chase gave a quick bow to the statue in reverence, but his mind was focused on his goal: To bring destruction to the world and set chaos free. True, the world was already going to hell in a hand basket as it was, but he was more than willing to help it along, and so were the others, especially if it included bringing Set forth and lining their pockets with wealth and power over the miserable wretches who'd survive.

Chase and his buddies were all parolees, as were most of the men in the cult, though they were lucky enough to have some wealthier members who helped finance their enterprise. Chase had read quite a bit about the Egyptian gods while in the state penitentiary for gang activity, and he was excited by the idea of a world filled with chaos, making his own crimes less noticeable. When he discovered a particular tome with virtual step-by-step instructions on how to bring about the world's unrest, he simply couldn't resist getting his fellow inmates, gang members, and anyone else with an interest in universal discord involved. It'd take an army to bring the world governments down, and one led by a god couldn't help but succeed. With the bureaucracies dealing with social turmoil, everyone in the cult would stand to accrue financial status and power, having laid the foundation in preparation for such an event.

Chase set the satchel containing the ornate box on the altar with deferred reverence and moved quickly to don a black robe more elaborate than the mundane brown ones hanging against the wall. His was made of satin, adorned with glyphs and designs honoring Set. On the back was an embroidered replica of the statue in the hangar. Flipping the hood up, Chase moved to the table and pulled out the book he used as reference. The box was just as it was described. Inside, he should find the ultimate article for good and justice. However, the artifact, whatever it was, needed to be destroyed with a ceremony that included a sacrifice. He had no problems with killing, especially when it could benefit him greatly. The others in the cult were a means to an end. He'd become so focused on achieving his goal, little else mattered. He would see it done, regardless of who or what it cost to succeed.

As Chase admired the box, he couldn't help

remembering when he first saw it. Originally, Chase didn't know how to achieve setting Set free and bringing about the destruction of world governments until he had a dream from the god himself, informing him where the desired object could be found. In his dream, he stood in front of the statue praying and suddenly the alabaster lips began to move. "I'll give you what you desire if you free me onto this world," Set's voice rumbled like low thunder.

"How do I release you?"

An image of the box appeared to float before him. "I will make arrangements to have this object available to your human hands. I'll give you the time and place to locate it, but you will only have a short window in order to retrieve it. If you fail to obtain it when I tell you to, you will lose your only opportunity to prove yourself worth of my love. What is in the box is your true goal. The ritual to let me enter your human plane of existence is found in the book that first influenced you to my altar."

"I understand, my lord. I'll do as you bid and I'll succeed."

Chase didn't know the details of how it would get to the museum at such a specific day and time, or why there was such a tight window of opportunity to retrieve it, but as he didn't tell Jones or the Bond brothers every intimate detail of their jobs, he assumed the god would only tell him what he needed to know. And he was okay with that. He figured the object would be on the plane of existence with the gods themselves. He also assumed Set would make arrangements to have it stolen and placed somewhere that would make it accessible to him. How ironic the fates would bring it to the city he lived in instead of his having to travel gods knew where to get it. It made things so much easier, because here he had a safe place to stash the item. In Chicago he could make the proper arrangements to have it snatched and knew the guys he employed. Yes, convenient. He was also informed he had just a little over one week left to do the ceremony. Originally, he had two weeks from the time it was stolen, but it took almost a week for it to be discovered and delivered to the museum for them to retrieve it. There weren't too many days left. Time was of the essence.

Now, just as his dream predicted, he held the desired commodity between his greedy hands. Chase carefully opened the box to see what he would find inside, not sure what to expect. When he saw the ornate ostrich feather, he was bewildered at first. A feather? What the fuck did the feather of a flightless bird have to do with the power of good? Then Chase remembered some of the other legends he'd read. Ma'at used a feather to weigh the hearts of those deceased to see if they were virtuous in life in order to pass into the world of Osiris, aka Heaven. Chase realized if the object were destroyed, so would any chance the world had for peace. A sinister smile spread across his face as several ideas ran through his head of whom he'd offer up in sacrifice to complete the ceremony for world destruction in the name of Set. So many came to mind immediately. Past snitches that put him in jail, the lawyers and judges who condemned him of breaking the rules of society. Honestly, he didn't care who would get chosen eventually. That wasn't his concern. Completing the ritual successfully was all that mattered.

Chapter 7

The surveillance tapes of the museum didn't provide much information. The four men were hooded. Other than identifying the tallest as the leader, pointing what to do and not speaking, there was little they could discern. The men knew what they wanted, where it was located, and how to get it, and for the most part, they avoided the cameras, which were unable to obtain anything useful, even when the cameras did catch glimpses of them. The leader did have a tattoo on his hand, and when the tech blew it up, Asim snarled.

"That's Set's emblem."

Lyra frowned and glanced over at Bas. It was what Asim had feared the most, and from their discussion last night, Set's minions had a good chance of succeeding if they didn't hurry. Bas nodded and stepped out of the room. They had discussed what to do in case the feather was taken before they could get it. Bas was going to check with some of his sources to see if they knew of a cult of Set. If they were lucky, they might find where the headquarters were located and get the feather back before the ceremony to destroy it permanently.

Lyra felt an intense anxiety to get the feather, a feeling of being immensely responsible for the entire situation. All she'd wanted was to prove Horemheb had offspring. It was what pushed her through her studies, what guided her to her excavations and research, and what influenced her continued pursuit despite the ridicule of her colleagues. After her parents' deaths, it was the one thought that propelled her out of her depression, a focus which galvanized her to action. A sense of purpose to prove her hypothesis was now overshadowed by something more important. The fate of the world rested on her, Bas, and Asim. Nothing else mattered—nothing else could.

While Bas went to check with his sources about the cult, she decided to check with the cameras outside the John G. Shedd Aquarium and Soldier Field. Maybe one of their cameras had picked up something the Field's exterior cameras didn't. After a few phone calls and explanations, Soldier Field called them back to say they thought they might have something. Lyra and Asim quickly headed over to the Soldier Field security office to see what was uncovered.

As soon as they entered the building, S.O. Mick Nesburn greeted them. "Ms. Mayet?"

Lyra nodded and pointed to her companion. "This is Asim, the Egyptian delegate for the new exhibit that was broken into this morning. Thank you for helping us try to obtain info on these culprits who robbed the museum earlier today. The E.M.A. would have a conniption if they knew about this, so if we can recover it before it becomes an international issue, you'll have saved relations between us, and my butt as well."

Mick chuckled. "Such a cute butt, too. Anything I can do to help save it is my pleasure. Follow me. I'll show you what we've got and see if it helps." Mick led the way down a couple of halls. Lyra followed, although she felt Mick was very unprofessional. She needed whatever he found on the tapes, so remained quiet.

Asim took the rear for three different reasons: One, it bothered him that Mick mentioned her ass. Yeah, it was very nice, but *he* didn't need to talk about it. Which brought him to the second reason— he had a nice vantage point to enjoy the sway of her hips as she walked with him behind. Finally, following allowed him to hide the slight growth of his organ and the opportunity to adjust his cock in the process without being noticed. The tightness of the jeans he wore from Bas didn't help the constriction much, though. His own attire hid his desire much better than the denim did.

Entering the small office with several televisions, they saw one monitor was already queued up and paused, showing a white van on the screen. Mick pointed to the display and started the video. It was pretty much what they had seen from the museum's surveillance. A white van, the front and back plates obscured with mud to prevent them from being identified. Lyra became deflated. "We've got the same thing."

"Do you?" Mick asked. "So, you saw the small emblem?"

Lyra perked up. "Emblem?"

Mick smiled. "Yeah. Hold on." While Mick punched a few keys on the keyboard, he tossed back, "I think you might owe me a dinner for this."

"Is that your way of asking me out?" Lyra said as she moved closer to the screen to better see the first possible real clue they might have.

Asim snarled, "She's taken."

Lyra gasped slightly as she straightened up to gaze wide-eyed at him. He gave her a look that brooked no nonsense, and she figured it was his way of letting her know they would talk about it later. The fact he thought there was something to talk about sent a thrill of excitement through her, and her mind instantly went to last night's activities. Remembering the feel of his lips pressed against hers, his hard body and strong arms wrapped around her, set her blood on fire and she had to force herself to focus on the task at hand. She turned back to Mick, who now had zoomed in on the emblem. There, on the corner of the van, was a small, very faded silhouette of an airplane and the letters C.O.A.A. in a circle around it. It wasn't noticeable on the museum's video because of the angle. It was only momentarily visible on Soldier Field's because of the three-point turn the van had needed to make in order to leave the area. With excitement, she hugged Mick and thanked him profusely for the lead.

Asim fought to remain stoic, not letting his possessive anger take hold when what he really wanted to do was claim her for himself, just as he had Namire. He had no right. He knew he didn't. Hell, he didn't even know if she felt the same. She might think of him as nothing more than a physical distraction to alleviate her boredom, a guy she was obligated to work with until he got the feather back, and then she could put him out of her mind. Maybe she was interested in Mick or Bas, or any number of other men. He was a huge fool. What right did he have to say she was taken just because *he* wanted her?

The world had changed since he was with Namire. Women had changed. They were stronger, more independent. True, it was one of the things he had admired about Namire, but thousands of years ago that was the exception, not the norm. Today, it was different. Still, something about Lyra seemed to set her apart. He wanted to touch her. To kiss her again. Fuck, he wanted to all-out claim her in every way possible. He wanted to feel that gorgeous ass in his hands, taste her nipples and make them hard with his tongue, feel her wetness against his fingers, and appease the ever-growing ache in his loins.

Lyra pulled out her phone and started to look for the symbol online while they walked back to the exit. Once outside, she turned to Asim. "I found the symbol belonging to an old hangar on Route 59. It will take us about an hour or so to get there, depending on traffic. Should we call for the police? I was thinking if we involve them, we'd have the box confiscated for evidence, and considering you mentioned there was a time limit in getting it returned to Ma'at, it might not be the best course of action. What are your thoughts?"

Asim tried to concentrate on her words, but her body was his main focus at the moment. He couldn't get her subtle movements out of his head and suddenly couldn't seem to see anything else but her. What was wrong with him? He had a job to do that was more important than his lust for a beautiful woman. However, truth be told, it was more than lust. He enjoyed talking to her, listening to her, being with her. She reminded him of Namire, but with differences—stronger, more independent—qualities he admired in her. She was talking to him about the symbol Mick had discovered on his video and it took a moment for her words to register. "We can't risk having it fall into anyone else's hands. Not even the police. We're running out of time to return it to Ma'at."

"That was my thought, too. Let me talk to Bas and see what he's got. Let him know what we found, and I'll talk to Henry to borrow his car. Then we can head out there and at least size up the situation."

"I can handle almost anything."

"I'm sure you can, Asim, but it'd be better to investigate before dashing in recklessly against untold creatures."

He lifted his head pridefully at the insinuation of being brash. "I'm not reckless. I'm confident I can deal with a handful of humans. I've led armies into battle for centuries against far worse."

"I'm sorry. I didn't mean to be disrespectful. I just want to be cautious. See what we're dealing with. If we just barge in, we might be walking into a trap or something."

"I highly doubt it can be anything I'll be unable to handle."

Lyra pressed her lips together. Continuing to argue was pointless and they were wasting time. She re-entered the Field Museum and found Bas, then Henry. She had to keep Bas from joining them because they needed him to run interference and deal with the destruction of the lab, cataloguing what was still there and trying to put the room back into a workable semblance of order to give them a head start before the police were called in. Henry wasn't thrilled to loan his car, but her insistence caused him to hand over the keys just to end her pestering.

Keys in hand, Lyra led Asim out to Henry's '02 blue Toyota RAV4. She pulled the GPS up on her phone and pulled out of the parking area along the lakefront, getting on 55 South. Asim had been quiet since leaving Soldier Field, and she worried she had insulted him. She'd no intention of being unkind to him. He had a heavy responsibility. From their discussions the previous evening, she was aware of the direness of the situation. Asim only had six more days to get the feather back into Ma'at's possession. If he failed, Ma'at's plume would disintegrate, and so would her magic. The world would be thrown into total chaos as easily as if it were purposefully destroyed in a ceremony. The time constraint alone had to be maddening, but add to it the weight of the consequences should he fail in his mission, she couldn't even imagine how anxious he must feel. She was also solicitous about not achieving their goal. But if she were truthful, she was also afraid she'd never see him again once his mission was complete.

"What did you mean by saying I was taken?" The sullen silence that hung between them was disrupted by her question.

Her words broke his reverie and he turned to her, contemplating his answer. He had begun to realize that once he achieved his goal he'd have to leave her behind. She wasn't some reward for him and she didn't belong in his world. He turned back to peer out the window. "I meant nothing. I felt he was being rude, and assumed if he knew you weren't available he might give you more respect."

"Oh." She was disappointed, but what could she say? He had a job and he made it painfully obvious she was a means to an end in achieving it. Last night happened because she prompted it, and no matter the reason, most men didn't think of it as much more than exercise. "According to the GPS, we should be at the hangar in about ten more minutes."

"Fine." He kept staring out the window. He'd never been outside of Egypt before, except when he was fighting a battle, and most of those hadn't existed after Queen Cleopatra's death when the Romans took over the land. There wasn't any need to explore, so he served Anubis and the other gods as needed. The land was occupied by other nations, but if the Egyptians didn't fight against them, there was little he could do. No matter who claimed Egypt as their own, there were always those who passed away and needed guidance to the underworld. Again, he wondered what life would've been like had Namire lived. One thing he knew for sure, he wouldn't have been lonely. His solitude had never bothered him much, at least not until he met Lyra. She seemed to make his reclusiveness more prominent. He found she was someone he looked forward to being with and talking to. She was a ball of energy and excitement he hadn't even realized he was missing until he was in her presence. Now he wondered how he was supposed to go back to his hermit existence.

He forced himself to pull away from the path his thoughts were on. He needed to focus and prepare for a possible confrontation to retrieve the feather. That alone was his singular goal. It was his duty. Before he knew it, she had stopped the vehicle and pointed. "According to my information, that's the old hangar. I figured it best to park back here so we wouldn't give away our approach, just in case they're in there."

"*Our* approach?" He turned to her, a frown giving him a dark look. "You're not going anywhere near that building. I'll check it out, and if I find the feather, I'll let you know I've got it."

"And what exactly am I supposed to do in the meantime?"

"Stay here and out of the way."

Lyra almost sputtered in her sudden anger. "Out of the way? You'd not even be here if it weren't for me."

"If it weren't for you, the feather would still be in Namire's tomb, where humans couldn't have gotten it but I could've," he snarled.

"So, what? You're saying I helped them by taking it out of the tomb? That they knew it would be there, so that's where it was hidden so I could get it into human hands? Is that what you're implying?" She was flabbergasted and annoyed. She couldn't believe he'd think she had anything to do with its original theft.

Asim pulled back slightly. She brought up something he hadn't considered before. Who was really behind the original theft, and who hid it in a secured location? Only someone who carried magic could infiltrate both areas: Ma'at's chambers and Namire's resting place. Who put things in motion, knowing Namire's tomb would be discovered and the feather would then be accessed by humans? What were the plans for that feather? If it was just to destroy it, they could've done that when it had first been taken. It meant whoever took the feather had a greater purpose for it. A ritual would be the only thing that made sense. Would bringing about chaos be the only agenda, or was something more planned? Were they hoping to bring back Set himself? Or Apep? Opening the door for either or both of them to walk among the hell they would bring?

"No. I think you were manipulated into retrieving the feather, but if it hadn't been you, it would've been someone else. Some other way to get the feather into human hands. However, you don't know what forces you'll be up against, and I won't risk you being hurt trying to do my job. You'll stay here, or I'll make you stay here. Is that understood?"

Lyra wanted to protest, but she knew in her heart he was right. How could she combat mystic forces? She'd be in his way more than anything. Besides, it was easier to agree and sneak a peek than to argue with him. She'd do it anyway and avoid the arguing part. "I understand," she relented weakly, knowing it would sell better if he thought she had given in to his demands.

He slipped out of the vehicle and gave her a last warning look before he dashed toward the building. She watched him until he slipped inside and she couldn't see him any longer. She sat in the RAV4, counting slowly to one hundred. She figured at that point enough time had passed. She got out of the car, looking around carefully before crossing to the building. She had paid attention to how Asim had gotten in, and she planned to mimic his movements. She'd barely entered when two men appeared on either side of her. Both were draped in brown robes, but their hoods were pushed back. She struggled and was about to scream when she felt a pinch on her arm and suddenly everything in her line of vision got blurry and dark. Then, nothing.

Erik stepped back and let David catch her as she collapsed. "Fuck, that shit works fast. She didn't even have a chance to scream."

David scooped her up, flinging her over his shoulder in a fireman's carry. "You should consider getting some of that for your old lady when she's on one of her rampages."

"I tried, and Chase nearly took my head off when he noticed some was missing."

"Shit, bro. I was fucking with you. Didn't expect you to actually do it."

"Megan is getting pretty bitchy lately. I figured if I could shut her flytrap for even just a couple of hours, I might be able to continue dealing with her." Erik held the door open for David and the load he carried. Once inside the spacious room, they headed toward the altar and set Lyra down.

"When do the others get here?" David asked.

"They should be arriving within the hour. Chase said he had some special wards and stuff he needed to do to prepare."

"You think he's taking care of the dude that came in earlier?"

"I'd assume so, since we were only sent to take care of her. I'm glad she came in, though. I didn't relish going outside to drag her in. This was much easier." Erik stepped forward and secured Lyra onto the altar's table. "Wonder how he knew they were coming."

"If you ask him, he'd say the statue told him. Chase is such a loon. But, he pays good, so I don't really care what he believes." David secured her other side and frowned as he stepped back once they were finished. "Fucking shame," he mumbled. "She's not too hideous."

"She's not awake, either, so she hasn't opened her mouth. Megan is great to look at, but a bitch otherwise. Although, she's fucking great in bed. Mainly why I keep her around."

"I was kinda wondering, bro. But you can get sex anywhere without the hassle."

Erik shook his head. "Not really. Megan is fucking wild in bed and so much fun, I don't think I could give it up, regardless of her fucking mouth."

"You're so whipped, bro. So whipped."

Erik punched David between the shoulder blades. "You're such an ass."

"Have you decided on a tattoo yet? I know you've been talking about getting a new one on your arm."

Erik shook his head. "Can't decide. The old

lady wants me to put something of her there, but fuck if I know what that won't make me look like some pansy."

"You should put a toilet there. Cause like, you're the shit, dude."

Erik took a step to chase him and beat the crap out of his brother, but was interrupted.

Chase came up behind them. "If you two are done playing around, there are those boxes that need to be brought in for the ceremony."

Erik scowled at David and turned without a word to get the boxes from the other room. David sullenly followed, throwing one last glance at Lyra, who was still unconscious. He had the errant hope that maybe Chase would let him play with her once Chase was done with her for whatever purpose he planned on.

Chapter 8

Osiris paced the receiving chamber while his wife, Isis, and Ma'at sat quietly watching him. They were waiting for Anubis to arrive and see what, if anything, had been discovered about the culprit of the theft. They were all keenly aware it had to be someone within their own pantheon, for only they would've had access to Ma'at's Temple and the location of the feather. Anubis had also heard from Asim that the feather had been placed in a tomb that was being excavated. With that kind of news, the gods knew that whoever stole the feather was also aware of the excavation and, using their celestial powers, would be able to enter the final resting place to position the feather inside without disturbing anything else, so as to have the plume found when the excavation was completed. It was a sneaky way to secure the feather within the human plane of existence and keep themselves from tipping their hand too soon.

Osiris and Ma'at tried to remember Namire, the woman whose tomb the feather had been secreted to, but so many centuries had passed, so many came before them to be judged, they couldn't quite pinpoint her specifically. At least, not until Anubis reminded them that she was Horemheb's daughter and was stoned to death because of her liaison with his beta, Asim.

Their reverie was soon disrupted when the chamber doors crashed open and they all looked up towards the disturbance. Anubis threw a huge giant snake onto the floor at Osiris' feet. Osiris scowled as Bast and Sekmet both followed Anubis inside the chamber. Bast, the beautiful, serene, cat goddess pulled on the cord wrapped around the serpent's neck while Sekmet, the golden lion goddess, brandished her sword to keep the slithering giant tame.

"What's the meaning of this?" Osiris glared at the situation taking place before him.

"Apep has continued his battle of late. He is the one who stole Ma'at's feather and hid it in Namire's tomb to be discovered by the humans."

"And you have proof of this?" Ma'at asked as she approached the immense twenty-foot slithering god.

Apep was once a sun god until Ra came onto the scene. Then Apep shifted to a god of evil and darkness who battled daily to keep Ra from bringing the dawn of day. When he would win the battle, the day would be cloudy and filled with storms. He was also associated with chaotic events, like eclipses, earthquakes, and more. A child of Neith, the goddess of the hunt and war, as well as brother to Ra and others, Apep hated how he was pushed aside for Ra and swore revenge for being mostly ignored or cursed. Never defeated, he could be slowed down temporarily. Now, it appears, he's come back with a vengeance.

"Tell them!" Anubis commanded. He had enlisted Bast and Sekmet before he went after Apep, knowing the felines would be able to control him the best since they were natural enemies with centuries of battles between them.

The snake hissed at Anubis, but when the two

women moved into his line of sight he curled up. His height had him looking down onto Osiris and the others, but the felines could still kick his ass and he was well aware of it. Originally, he had planned on remaining silent, but he couldn't help boasting a bit about his success in the theft. "I sssstole the fffeather. Tired of being pussshed assside. Time for chaosss to win for a change. Time for chaosss to ssshine." Apep showed his fangs as he spoke.

Ma'at stood, unafraid of Apep as she glared up into his face. Even though she didn't have her famous bibelot, she was still able to derive the power of justice by compelling Apep to tell the truth. "Why now, after all of these centuries? We no longer have the powers we once did, overlooked in this modern world as nothing more than interesting oddities."

Coerced to explain his actions, Apep explained, "Becaussse the time wasss right. I knew it would be found by humansss and given to one who knew what to do with it to make the mossst of itsss power and your weaknesss. It'sss time for a new age to come. A time for chaosss to reign. Your time isss over."

"Did you work alone?"

"No. I had human help."

"Just humans?"

"Maybe. Maybe not. Only I know for sssure."

Ma'at peered into his eyes and repeated the question. "Just humans?"

"No. Another came up with the idea."

"Who?"

Apep struggled in responding, but Ma'at's

powers were still strong. He knew she was running out of time before her powers would weaken and subside, but at the moment she was still impressively influential. He barely realized he spoke until it was too late. "Ssssset."

Osiris rubbed his head and gently pulled Ma'at back towards Isis. The damage had been done, the catalyst started, thanks to the god of darkness and chaos. The only thing they could do now was to hope Anubis' beta found the feather in time and stopped the progression from concluding with the loss of all goodness in the world.

"Take Apep away. You know what to do."

Anubis nodded as Bast and Sekmet pulled and prodded Apep's removal from the chamber. Apep's son, Thoth, had a book of spells that would keep Apep contained. The book revealed Apep's list of secret names, as well as several hymns which reflected Ra's victories, making Apep weak. By maintaining the serpent's feebleness, they'd ensure he wouldn't be a further nuisance.

"You can try to keep me sssedated, but the wheelsss have been put into motion. You cannot ssstop what will occur and Ma'at will be no more," Apep called out as he was dragged away, the silence descending upon the room once the chambers' doors were shut.

Osiris glanced over at Ma'at. "I think it best that you find Asim and remain close so there is no further delay once the feather is located. Now that we know who's behind the original theft, we need to deal with the consequences. Apep doesn't have much of a following anymore and I feared someone else was aiding him. Set, is of course, the logical choice. Albeit, the only proof we have is Apep's confession."

Ma'at stood, only to bow low. "As you command." She then disappeared from the chambers. Just because they knew Apep stole the plume didn't mean it was safe. They were still on a time limit. A very dangerous game had been set into motion. She wondered if Apep really understood the ramifications of his actions.

Alone again, Osiris moved over to Isis and rested his head against her shoulder. He knew she alone was aware of the heavy toll these recent events placed upon him, but he never showed his deepest concerns to any save her. He knew he could trust her since she did everything to put him back together after Set slayed and dismembered him, scattering his body parts across the land and sea of Egypt. He could only hope Asim would succeed in time.

Ma'at appeared in a darkened room, the scent of Asim strong. Hearing a noise behind her, she turned around to see a man she didn't recognize using a towel to dry his hair as he walked out of the bathroom wearing nothing at all but a few drops of water upon his glistening skin. The towel was over his head as he rubbed his shoulder-length hair dry. He had not noticed her as of yet and, for the moment, she was perfectly fine in keeping it that way. His distraction gave her the opportunity to stare at him. She had seen many gods, and they were all perfect, but to see this human male in all his glory, she couldn't help but wonder what she might have been missing all these centuries. She spent most of her time in the underworld waiting for human souls to come to her for judgment. By the time those humans reached her, they bore little appeal to her. She hadn't seen a live human male in eons and this one before her was far more than she expected. Thoughts of feeling his hard, ripped abs under her fingers was foremost in her thoughts and she almost forgot why she was in the human world to begin with. Oh, it had been far too long since she gave herself to the carnal pleasures of the flesh and she felt slightly moistened at the thought of being with this human. But this was neither the time nor place for such indulgences. She focused on her duty and wondered why he was here and naked, especially when Asim's scent was so strong, yet he didn't seem to be around.

Snarling, she caught him off guard as he looked up from under the towel in surprise, suddenly realizing he wasn't alone. He didn't even have time to cover himself or react in any other way as the woman suddenly, and with a force belying her petite stature, slammed him up against a wall, a tight hand around his throat.

Bas gripped the woman's slender fingers, trying to pry them off him. He had no idea who this woman was or why she was here. He just knew his air was running out and his legs were on tip toes. Worse, he couldn't seem to break free. He wasn't a weak man, but between Asim and now this small wisp of a woman, he was beginning to doubt his own manhood!

"What have you done to him?"

"Him?" Bas gasped, still tugging at his throat to breathe. He couldn't think beyond much else other than the extreme will to live and the fear he was about to die by a woman's hand while totally nude. How undignified! Talk about a major blow to his masculinity.

She seemed to know she was killing him and lowered him to the ground, as well as loosened her overtly tight grip on his throat. "Asim. Where is he?"

"What the hell, lady?" Bas continued to struggle, not even caring he was bare-ass naked, yet unsure who she even was to consider divulging such information as Asim's whereabouts so effortlessly.

"Tell me now, or suffer the consequences."

"Look, he ain't here. Do you see him? No. 'Cause he ain't here."

"Then where is he?"

"And why should I tell you shit?"

"Because you will die if you don't, and since I weigh the hearts, yours will be found extremely heavy, just for getting me upset."

Her words sank in and he blinked in shock at her. Suddenly, her Egyptian-garbed appearance, her asking about Asim, and her strength made sense, in as much as anything else these past couple of days. Things he never believed could be real were making their way known in his previously limited world. "You're telling me you're Ma'at?"

She tilted her head at his words, her face remaining stoic. "So, you have heard of me."

"Yeah. It's your freaking feather me and my colleague are looking for with Asim."

"If you are working with him, where is he?"

"He and Lyra are checking out a lead."

She loosened her grip, finally releasing him. He rubbed his throat, but still didn't bother covering himself. "Why is his scent so strong here if he is not here himself? Who is Lyra?"

He looked at her, puzzled, then dawning appeared in his gaze. "I loaned him some clothes yesterday. He changed them and threw them in a pile over there. That is probably what you are sensing." Bas pointed to a pile of clothes on the floor by the hamper. *I knew I was going to have to burn them. Lyra now owes me new clothes!* His thoughts made him grumble his response to the goddess. "Lyra is the archeologist who found the feather and brought it here. To Chicago. In the United States. It was stolen while in transit and they are following up on a lead as to who might have absconded with it. "He couldn't believe he was telling her so much, but he was unaware that even without the feather she was still able to compel others to confess the truth.

As she turned to examine the haphazardly discarded clothes closer, she threw back, "You really should cover yourself." Not that she minded his nudeness. He was definitely a pleasure to look at, but it also distracted her on why she was here.

"Yeah, I probably should, but you're the one who barged in here, so you can suffer while I dry off and get dressed. I only came back for a quick shower and change of clothes to get out of the ones

I wore for two days on the train. Lyra is with Asim working on an angle to your missing feather, and I'm waiting for some phone calls to be returned before I meet up with her and Asim."

Ma'at bent down and picked up the pile of clothes, sniffing them, then let them drop where they had lain. She turned to him, her eyes going over his hard body once again. His abs were like a washboard, his shoulder-length, blondish hair was plastered against his neck from his shower, but even still, she could see the golden highlights the strands contained. Shame she wasn't here for him. She could see a multitude of ways to enjoy his flesh. Maybe she would indulge herself if she survived this ordeal. If the feather remained lost, it wouldn't matter, for she'd wither and die. Already there were moments of weakness. She knew they would only worsen when the clock ran out on getting it returned to her. Her powers were only good as long as the feather existed. She ignored the lightheadedness she suffered on occasion. She had to get the sacred plume back and time was growing short. "What name are you known by?" she asked.

"Bas."

She snorted with laughter. "You're nothing like the cat goddess."

He sneered. "I'm very aware of that. It's short for Sebastian."

"Sebastian. I like that better. It suits you more."

He pulled on his pants as he gave her a sideways glance. "You can call me that if you prefer." Other than the fact she almost strangled him to death, he couldn't help but admire her beauty. Her skin was creamy, her eyes slanted and dark. Her hair was a dark, shiny brown and he was sure it was as soft as silk. He found himself wanting to touch it, but he realized the foolishness of that idea. It would be his luck he would let his hand feel those luscious tendrils and she would find it insulting and blast him to kingdom come as a result. She held herself regally and with purpose. She was the first woman since Lyra that actually made his heart race, albeit he wasn't sure it wasn't solely from his almost dying at her hand. Pulling a polo over his head, he grabbed his phone and keys. "Look, if you want, you're welcome to come with me. After a bit, I'll probably be meeting up with him and my friend."

Ma'at gazed at him, watching his every movement. She couldn't believe he was solely human. He didn't seem to care she was a goddess or that she dealt with the dead daily. He talked to her as if they were equals and she appreciated it. Plus, the way he moved, his taut muscles rippling with every stretch or pull he made to get dressed, thrilled her beyond her wildest imagination. Sure she could just disappear as quickly as she appeared, but the idea of spending more time with this human enticed her and she couldn't resist giving in to her desire.

"I agree to your proposition."

Bas peered closely at her. His eyes traveling down and up her body slowly, taking in every aspect of her. "You should at least remove your collar. It's a little too much for this day and age. Women wear maxi dresses all the time of late, so the rest is fine." Although he wanted to make sure she would fit in a bit better so as to not raise suspicion, he couldn't help but notice her rounded curves. He wondered what she would look like naked with a soft glow to highlight her skin. He wondered how a goddess would taste under his tongue. He wondered what she would do to him if he didn't please her, and he quickly looked away after his comments. "Good. Come on." He held the door open for her as he ushered her out of his home.

Chapter 9

Asim managed to sneak into the warehouse and successfully avoid the men moving about. It was an odd place. A couple of offices, a few closed doors, which would need to be investigated later, and a stairway that led up to who knew what. His canine abilities crossed over when he was in human form. Centuries of utilizing his powers had given him the ability to hone them without having to be in jackal form. He was stealthy, using his nose to detect where the humans were to better avoid them. What his nose didn't pick up, his hearing would. After a couple of men came down from the upper floor, Asim hopped over the banister and proceeded to climb the stairs quickly in order to search for the feather in what he assumed would be a secure location. His senses were on high alert as he looked for the ornate box or any sign of the sacred plume itself.

He could tell the men were busy, moving things about. They certainly weren't discreet in their movements. Quite the contrary—they sounded like a herd of elephants stomping about. It made keeping track of them easy. His search, though, was proving futile.

He was about to head out of the office and lounge area when he heard someone approaching. Shifting quickly, he sat in the corner while a scruffy tattooed and bearded man entered.

Virgil stopped and looked at Asim, scratching his hairy chin. He didn't remember a jackal statue in the corner. It was big, almost life-sized. Had it been there long? His brown eyes darted about as he looked for anything else he might've missed and hadn't realized. Giving his head a shake, he headed to the safe on the wall and pulled out his wallet where he had a small piece of paper with the combination on it. Referring to it, he opened the safe and took out the ornate box Asim had been looking for. Quickly closing the safe, Virgil ran out the doorway and down the stairs, whisking the door closed behind him.

Asim shifted from statue to life, but Virgil was out the door as Asim was mid-leap on his attack. Asim landed on all fours, staring at the closed door. Virgil never even suspected he had come to life and was about to be jackal kibble. Asim would've taken the container from his greedy little hands, and his mission would've been accomplished. Of course, it wasn't going to be that easy. Why should he have ever thought it would be so simple? Moving onto his hind legs, Asim shifted from jackal into human in the blink of an eye, minus Bas' clothes and in his own comfortable, yet more exposed, Egyptian wear.

He had a single goal: to get that box back. He flung open the door and ran down the stairs just as Virgil disappeared through a door along the back wall. Any sense of being stealthy evaporated the moment he realized how close he was to completing his assignment. He flung the door open without thought. No matter how many humans he had to face, he'd had worse odds. There was a time he had stood among thousands of men on a battlefield and defeated them all. He had no problem fighting, and killing, if need be to win. He would, after all, be saving millions as a result of any action he took. The outcome would outweigh the few deaths he might have to inflict here.

The sight that greeted him, however, was nothing like he expected or was prepared for. He stopped short, taking everything in, his mouth slightly ajar in order to take in some air since his nose had forgotten how to do so.

The converted hangar was filled with a dozen robed figures, hoods pulled over their faces, casting them in shadows. Opposite the entryway was a huge twenty-foot statue of Set. But what caught Asim's eyes the most was the black-robed figure on the pedestal where an altar stood, with a bound, wide-eyed, gagged and struggling Lyra.

It was almost as if they were expecting him. They all turned and faced Asim, causing Lyra to see what inspired her momentary reprieve.

Never had anyone looked more heroic than Asim the moment her eyes landed on him. Of course, the lack of outfit didn't detract from the relief she felt at seeing him. He would save her. She wasn't sure how, only that he would. A heavy thudding sound behind the head priest caused everyone to turn their focus upon the statue. A dull, hazy outline around the figure could be seen.

Chase waved Virgil over, literally pulling the box from his grasp to open it. Inside lay the Feather of Ma'at, the emblem for good and justice, the antithesis of everything Apep and Set stood for. Chase was aware of what Set had gone through to get the feather this far. Set had convinced Apep to steal the feather and set it in some tomb that was currently being excavated. Chase had seen the entire plan of the feather's theft in the dreams Set sent him. He knew of everything that had occurred in order to get the feather here to use it in the ceremony that would allow Set the freedom to enter this human world. Once free of his confines, Set would initiate the end of the world as we knew it. He would overrun the governments and establish himself to be worshipped. He would oversee the death of those who refused to accept Set as their god and Chase as his right-hand man. Chase would get all the power he so desperately desired, as well as the recognition he'd fought for. He'd be able to live his life in pure luxury and he'd do it for eternity, for he'd become immortal as his reward for releasing Set. His heart beat rapidly in anticipation of the culmination of his efforts and desires.

The ceremony had started, so their time now was even more limited to bring forth the god than the two weeks they had originally been given. The doorway for Set had been opened slightly from the incantation spoken while Virgil was retrieving the box containing the treasured feather. Set was preparing to step through and lead his dark minions into the human realm. Only the worshippers inside the hangar would be safe from the wrath about to be unleashed on the unsuspecting world. Chase wasted no time. He was well aware the other worshippers would prevent the new person from stopping him while he used the feather to sacrifice Lyra, the final step to complete Set's entrance.

Chase knew the ceremony would require a dark deed in the name of the god to come forth. Blood needed to be spilled, the feather needed to be desecrated, and the incantation had to be chanted in order to open the portal needed for chaos to spread its wings and decimate the world. Chase used the ceremonial knife to slice down the middle of Lyra's shirt, exposing her. Chase heard a scuffle on the floor, but he concentrated on the sacred words as he opened the box and removed the magical ostrich plume. He focused solely on his job, knowing the others would do theirs to keep the Egyptian from stopping him and the ceremony. Chase started reciting from the tome as he lifted the feather over Lyra's chest. The feather had a gold tip used to balance the weight on the scales when judging, but in this instance, it would be the metal to pierce her heart. Just as he was about to lower it and solidify the entrance for Set, his arm was jarred and he almost lost his grip on the feather.

Asim had realized what the head priest was doing the moment he saw Set's outline against the statue. Lyra was to be sacrificed to open the doorway. He couldn't let it happen. It was then he admitted to himself a truth he had been denying for the past two days. It wasn't just to keep humankind safe, or the world protected—it was to save a woman he had fallen in love with. He was compelled to save Lyra.

Utilizing his jackal strength, he leaped past the multitudes of brown robes and pounced toward the deadly tipped feather, knocking it from the priest's hand. Asim knew he had a lot to deal with. It was more than just getting his hands on the feather and flashing out to give it to Ma'at. If he did that, he would be leaving Lyra alone and vulnerable. He shouldn't care about the fate of one woman, but he did. He failed once before, centuries ago, with Namire. Lyra stirred something inside him and he wouldn't abandon her to some unknown and possibly fatal outcome.

Asim reached for the feather. Just as he was about to grasp it, he was pulled back as a horde of brown robes and flailing limbs tried to restrain him. The head priest quickly regained his composure and, firmly gripping the feather, plunged it into Lyra's chest. The blood quickly seeped into the plumage. Asim howled as he realized he'd failed to save Lyra. His eyes turned black and he released the animal within. His battle techniques reigning, he tore through the dozen men as they tried to subdue him.

The blood from Lyra did the impossible, permeating through the plume as it turned from white to red, her life force draining as the object soaked it up. Asim could feel the doorway open further, Set ready to appear in this world. The men who would've been rewarded now lay still at his feet in a pile he hadn't seen since his ancient days of battle. Their blood dripped down Asim's face and chest, but he cared little for the stickiness of the sanguine liquid as he set his sights on the male in the black robes who'd brought all of this to bear. There was still a chance, albeit an extremely small one, to save everything. One opportunity to succeed in his mission and to save her. He wasted no time as he flung Chase so hard against the far hanger wall that the man collapsed as he slid to the floor with a distinct thud.

He pulled the feather out of Lyra before it was completely destroyed. Hopefully Ma'at could repair the damage done by the corruption made against the artifact. His attention was now on Lyra. He placed a couple of fingers against her neck to feel for a pulse. It was there, but slight. He wasn't sure what to do or who to call for help.

Anubis was suddenly beside him in answer to Asim's silent summons. With Anubis were Bast and Sekmet, the latter a lioness goddess who was a fierce warrior and would handle Set. While Bast was the normally gentler of the two feline goddesses, she could be just as ferocious in battle as Sekmet. Together, Bast and Sekmet headed toward the statue, their armored bodies ready to do battle. They crossed into the slight dimensional rift to face Set head on.

Although the ones in the hangar couldn't see what was occurring, they could hear the sounds of surprise from Set when he saw the two feline goddesses enter in order to confront him.

"What are you doing here?" a deep, rumbling, male voice exclaimed in surprise.

"We're here to protect Ma'at and keep you from entering the human world."

"I am too close to succeeding and, once I do, there is nothing you can do to stop me. I can feel the power of the doorway opening and the feather keeping me at bay diminishing. Soon, you will know you have lost this battle and the human world will be mine."

"Never," the two women said in unison before

the cacophony of conflict could be heard. Metal clanging, hissing, shouting, and the sounds of bodies crashing into each other were distinctive despite the fact they couldn't be seen.

Asim turned to Anubis knowing the feline women would be able to handle Set's emergence. His concern for the world evaporated once the small entourage disappeared into the other realm and he focused on Lyra's imminent demise. When the hangar's exterior door slammed opened and a couple rushed in, Asim was prepared to fight the two in order to further protect Lyra. He relaxed a bit as soon as he recognized the couple was Bas and Ma'at. Briefly, Asim wondered when the two of them had gotten together, but just as quickly he brushed the thought aside.

Ma'at approached the center altar and Asim. She quickly assessed the situation—the feline goddesses battling within the statue, which had become hazy do to the imminent appearance of Set; the sacrificial body of a woman on the altar, who was bleeding profusely; and her once-white feather corrupted by the woman's blood. The ritual had taken place and the only veil yet to be pierced was the actual death of the sacrifice. Ma'at held her hand out for her property. Asim relinquished it immediately. Once again in her grip, the plume returned to its normal pristine-white appearance, all aspects of attempted corruption disappearing once it was back within her grasp. Again in her possession, the inter-dimensional door also slammed shut, keeping this world safe for a little while longer and diminishing the sounds of hostility within the veil of the other dimension.

She bowed her head to Asim. "You've done well, beta of Anubis. I'll not forget your sacrifice or deed." She also gave Anubis a curt nod. She gazed at Lyra for a moment, frowning before she stepped back towards Bas. She kept the human male she was intrigued with away from the altar and Lyra, even though he tried to circumvent her to reach the podium. He had been slower compared to the speed of the goddess when she really wanted to move and he hadn't been able to get to the altar before she returned to his side and held him back. "They need time. Give it to them and I promise all will be well."

Bas wanted to pick up Ma'at and set her down behind him, but something about her tone caused him to accept her advice, despite his own reservations to the contrary. Instead, he wavered, shifting from one foot to the other as he remained back by the door. He decided to use the time to call 911.

Anubis tilted his head as he moved closer to Lyra. Standing over her, he breathed deeply, then stepped back. "You may proceed in what you were about to do."

Asim nodded. There was no reason to ask how Anubis knew what he'd been contemplating. Anubis was a god and Asim was fairly certain he was just as aware there wasn't much time left. Lyra was fading quickly and would soon be dead if Asim didn't move quickly. Asim climbed on top of Lyra, shifting into a jackal as he did so, and bit her. Her blood rushed into his mouth. He kept his fangs buried into her shoulder for a moment before he pulled back and lapped up the puncture to seal the wound. Asim then moved down Lyra's body to lick the puncture near her heart. He prayed it would work. He'd never changed anyone before; he'd had no reason to.

All the while, he heard Bas scream and curse, unsure of what was going on, but not appreciating a jackal biting and crawling all over Lyra's prone body. Asim ignored everything around him save Lyra. He had to save her. She was the only thing that mattered to him, and he'd give his own life if need be in order to see she had a full one of her own. His snout sniffed Lyra, his eyes focusing solely on her chest, watching it rise and fall with breath and hoping she'd continue to breathe with a firm steadiness. She had to survive. He wasn't sure how he'd deal with her death if he failed.

He hadn't realized he was still hovering above her until Anubis cleared his throat. "It will work. As promised, she has come back to you. You'll need to train her in her new-found abilities."

Asim jumped off Lyra, shifting into a man so he could hold her hand as he stood beside her. He gave a quick glance back at Bas and Ma'at, surprised the goddess seemed to be calming down Bas, talking softly to him. His eyes then scanned the bodies that were scattered about the hangar. In the distance, he could hear wailing sirens approaching. "What about them?"

Anubis waved his hand and all the corpses disappeared. A god's power was infinite.

"Nice." Asim admired Anubis' ability, even if he couldn't do something so easily himself. "What did you mean, she had come back to me as promised?"

"Do you not recognize her?"

Asim gazed down at Lyra again. The bit of familiarity he noticed from the very first moment he'd seen her only increased as he got to know Lyra more intimately, and it confused him. "She reminds me of Namire."

"That's because she *is* Namire."

"I don't understand, my lord."

"She's Namire reincarnated, as promised eons ago."

Realization dawned on Asim. There was more than just getting the feather back as to why he was sent on this mission. He was destined to meet her, given a second chance to make things right. It's why Lyra had been so drawn to Namire's tomb, why the feather had been hidden there once it was stolen, and why she accepted him so readily. He wondered if she knew she had been reincarnated. He had a lot of explaining to do, and he hoped she'd listen to him.

Anubis' head turned as the sirens became louder. "Others are coming. When you have talked to her, and you're convinced she's cared for, return to my temple and call for me then."

Asim nodded as Anubis shimmered away. He wasn't sure he could leave Lyra if she chose not to return with him to Egypt. He covered Lyra up by placing one of the discarded robes over her. He could hear the sirens as they approached the old building. Men with uniforms and guns entered first. When they assessed it was secure, Bas headed over to the man who appeared to be in charge. His uniform indicated he was a sergeant by the strips on his sleeves.

Bas quickly gave a description of what was going on, keeping the gods, including Ma'at, out of it as much as possible. He certainly didn't need to be taken away for a psych evaluation because he told them everything. He selectively told them the details he could safely get away with, pointing to Lyra as being the one to be looked after. He explained the men who were here and causing the trouble left when they heard the sirens. The sergeant asked for a description of the vehicles. "What did you see them depart in?"

Bas figured it best to send them on a wild goose chase. He was more interested in having the paramedics looking after Lyra than helping the police fill out their forms or stand around questioning them. "They were in a white, unmarked van. These were the same men who broke into the Field Museum earlier and it looked like the same vehicle they used for the robbery. The report is filed with the Chicago Police."

This caused the officers to rapidly depart, leaving the medical personal, as well as the sergeant, behind as the remainder of the police attempted to catch up to the fugitives, unaware they were all dead and only Anubis knew where he made them disappear to.

Asim remained by Lyra's side as she was beginning to wake up, trying to keep her calm as they were approached by the EMTs. Asim told her everything was okay now and she was safe. "Don't tell them anything. Say you were unconscious and just now woke up. If you tell them the truth, they won't believe you," he whispered to her.

"I was thinking the same thing. Last thing I need is a comprehensive visit to the psych ward. No thank you. I can do without that." Lyra tried to sit up, but Asim held a hand on her shoulder, indicating she should remain still.

Asim knew the EMTs would be confused as to why there was so much blood and no visible wounds on Lyra, but he could only hope they would think it belonged to one of those who attacked her, or even animal's blood spilled on her since it was obvious there was some sort of devilish ritual that occurred before they arrived. However, Asim also knew she'd soon be very ill as her body adjusted to the change he brought about in her in order to save her very life. Asim knew he was going to have to ask for assistance in preparing her for what she was about to face. As much as he hated to leave her side, Asim moved towards Bas to speak privately with him after the EMTs reached Lyra, effectively pushing him aside. When Ma'at saw Asim approach, she seemed to know it needed to be a conversation between the males and she quietly excused herself, letting Bas know she had to return to her realm to put the feather into a new safe and secure location.

Bas grabbed her hand, asking her to return when she was done. He wasn't quite ready to let the intriguing woman go if she was as interested as he seemed to think she was. She smiled and agreed to return to him when she completed her job. She stepped to a secluded location and dematerialized. With Ma'at gone, Bas turned his concern back towards Lyra as the EMTs surrounded her.

"Is she okay?" Bas watched the EMTs. He wanted to go to Lyra himself, but he didn't want to get in the way of the professionals.

"She is now, but we can't let them take her."

"What do you mean? Why not?"

"Because she was dying, and I had to save her life."

"I don't understand. Do you mean when you went jackal on her? When you fucking bit her? What the hell was that about?" Bas whispered harshly, so the remaining officer and paramedics wouldn't be too suspicious of their conversation.

"I did what I needed to do. I saved her life. However, what I did is going to be painful in a few hours, and the hospital won't understand, won't know how to take care of her. We need to go someplace private. Do you understand? Do you know where we can go? It's for her safety. I know you probably don't trust me after seeing me bite her, but I'm totally serious. I did it for her, but I need your help now. They can't take her to a hospital." Asim pleaded with Bas, then added softly with a desperation even he was surprised at, "Please. Please don't let them take her."

Bas was hesitant, but he looked at Lyra sitting up, shooing away the medical team trying to examine her. He'd have to trust Asim, as much as he didn't want to. "Yeah. Alright. I have a summer home half an hour away. It should be secure enough. I'll go get the car ready, you get her, and then you're going to explain this whole thing to me very, very slowly."

Chapter 10

Bas stood on the wraparound porch facing the lake as the sun began to rise. It'd been an extremely long night. He heard the door open and smelled the coffee before he turned around. Asim handed him a steaming mug of joe. "Is she really going to be okay?"

Lyra had only been asleep for the past hour or so, but Bas' mind was far too active for sleep. He couldn't stop thinking about everything he'd witnessed, including seeing Lyra turn into a jackal, so he'd stepped outside for some fresh air. He didn't seem to be able to keep his mind from reliving the last 24 hours, no matter how hard he tried. From the moment he met Ma'at in person, to the painful throes Lyra spent the night going through, was something his brain kept going over, like scenes from a bad movie or a song one just couldn't get out of their head, no matter how much they wanted to.

"The worst is over. Her body needed to adjust. I promise she'll never have to go through anything like that again. Plus, now she'll live a very long life. Surely you'll appreciate knowing she won't succumb to illness and death so easily."

"That's not necessarily a great thing. She'll outlive her friends, her coworkers, everyone she knows. She'll have to relocate every so often, so others don't suspect she isn't aging. I'm glad she won't get sick. She won't die from things like cancer or whatever, but she'll watch all those she cares about leave her, and she already had that happen in her life and didn't take it very well." Bas couldn't help but remember Lyra losing her parents on 9/11 and how devastated she was as a result. There were moments he didn't think she would even survive, her depression so severe. How was it going to be when she lived for centuries and all her friends passed away from age? How would she manage the despair she was going to feel when she had no one to pull her out of her lugubrious slump? "You didn't give her a choice in this."

"She'll have me, if she wants. No, I didn't give her a choice. What I gave her is life. I won't let her die. Not again."

"What do you mean, not again?" Bas gave him a bewildered look. Had he missed something? Had she died and he wasn't even aware? The thought made his stomach flip.

Asim took a sip from his cup and sat on the porch swing, debating how much to tell him. He realized Bas had the right to know, considering how concerned he was for her and how close the two of them seemed to be. Asim learned earlier that they had once dated, but felt their friendship more important than a sexual liaison. He also realized he should probably let Lyra tell him anything she wanted him to know after he told her, but truth was, a part of him wanted to have support when he informed her of her past life. Who better to give that support than someone she trusted immensely? Bas was the logical choice. "What I'm about to tell you, she doesn't know yet. Please let me tell her when the time is right. However, I'd like you to know so she has a confidant to disclose the information with and who is aware of what is going on."

"And when will you determine when the time is right? When are you planning on giving her this important piece of information you're about to share with me?"

"After she's made her choice as to how she wants to live. I don't want her to feel influenced, but she does have some important choices she is going to need to make, and she should be fully informed about them without prejudice."

"You mean, after you talk her into coming with you?"

"No. She'll choose to come with me of her own volition or she will choose to stay. It's why I don't want her to know what I'm about to tell you until after she has made her decision. I don't feel she should be influenced by it when making her choice. I don't want her to know everything just yet, in case it might persuade her one way or the other."

"She should have all the knowledge in order to make an informed decision."

"Normally, I'd agree with you. In this case, not so much."

"What are you hiding? What did you mean when you said not die again?"

Asim wasn't sure how to say it. The direct approach seemed the most logical and yet, even in his head he knew it'd be hard for them to accept. They might even think he was making it all up. Hell! He hadn't even allowed himself to consider the possibility until Anubis pointed out what was now obvious to him. He just assumed he cared about her because of her intelligence and certain similarities in mannerisms to Namire. He'd never even guessed there was a logical reason; at least logical in his mystical world. "Lyra is Namire. Reincarnated."

Bas dropped his mug, the handle breaking off, the liquid running down the edge of the porch onto the ground below. "How do you know? Are you sure? I mean, how is this even a possible consideration?" To say he was shocked would be an understatement.

"I think my mind suspected but wouldn't accept it. Anubis confirmed it, though."

"Anubis? You mean, like, the god of the dead?"

"The one and only. Yes. Since he is the god of the dead, as you say, he is able to see more than just the exterior of someone. He can see their soul and where it's been, as well as where it's going to be. He told me once I'd see Namire again. It'd been so long, I'd assumed he was just trying to comfort me in my grief over her loss. I'd no idea it was Lyra until he said something to me at the altar. Sometimes the things closest to you are the things you overlook."

Bas didn't say anything, letting it all sink in. By claiming Lyra as Namire, he was claiming her for himself and that upset him, but not the way he expected. He wanted Lyra to be happy in a way he couldn't seem to make her. Maybe this was why they hadn't been able to make a go of it. In her own way, she had been waiting for Asim to come to her.

"Well, shit." Bas rubbed his forehead, caring less about the broken mug or spilled beverage. What was that compared to the sense of loss he was feeling, the extreme changes that were about to occur. He worried about Lyra. She had lost so much; with her new abilities she would lose so much more and, on top of it all, she had to deal with a great amount of change, something Bas was fully aware she didn't deal with very well. Yet, he couldn't help the side thought of Ma'at. Would this mean he would get to see the goddess again? Although he didn't know how one related to the other, he did hope on seeing the vixen of a goddess once again. She had haunted his thoughts since the moment she suspended him up against his apartment wall. He couldn't seem to get her out of his mind. Even though he doubted they would ever see each other again, a part of him still hoped he would.

Bas rubbed his unshaven jaw. Asim could tell he was mulling over everything he'd said, and he could only assume how hard it was for one to hear something so fantastic, even after everything Bas had seen and experienced. Eons later, Asim could still remember how he felt when he came face to face with the god Anubis. Or how he felt when he was able to shift for the first time on his own. Even the powerful abilities he acquired still astounded him, so he totally understood what Bas might be feeling upon hearing such incredulities. "I comprehend how difficult this might—"

"Difficult?" Bas cut off Asim in mid-sentence. "You think this is difficult? This may be everyday shit to you, dude, but it's totally new to us mere mortals. Lyra hates change. She hates loss. She doesn't know how to deal with either one, and yet you've changed her into some creature, extended her life, and now are about to tell her that not only is she going to live forever and watch everyone she cares about die of old age, but that she's lived once before. And as your consort, no less. Yeah, this ain't difficult at all. It's freaking vexing. I can't do anything, and you ask me to wait before I can even tell her this." Bas scrubbed his whiskered face again. "Dude, I'm going to ask this only one time. Be good to her and let her know everything. Don't keep stuff from her. She needs time to adjust to things, especially major things like this. Give her time and don't expect miracles. If she doesn't choose you, if she freaks about being reincarnated, or being a jackal, or whatever it is she freaks out about, just be patient with her. Okay?"

"You've got me all wrong. I'd planned on no less than what you are asking. It's why I asked you not to tell her just yet. Let her choose where she wants to be and whom she wishes to be with. She is going to have enough to deal with in regards to being part jackal and having several new abilities. I'll teach her regardless, or find someone else to do it if she never wishes to see me again. I know I took her choice away. That wasn't fair of me, and yet I just couldn't let her die. I couldn't bear the thought of losing her that way. If she chooses to not be with me, that's one thing. At least she will still be alive to make her mark in this world. I just couldn't let her die." Asim almost pleaded for Bas's understanding. He cared for—no, in truth, he loved Lyra, and he refused to lose her like he did Namire. He would give her the world if she asked for it, but she had to be alive to ask. He wasn't about to see another person he fell in love with have their life stripped from them unnecessarily. Namire's death haunted him for centuries. There was no way in hell he would live another multitude of centuries being haunted by the death of Lyra. He had to save her, and he did. He wasn't going to be sorry for it, but he understood what Bas was implying. He'd felt the same once about Namire. He felt that way now about Lyra. Bas just had to believe him; believe he was giving Lyra the chance to be the best she could be.

"Okay, Asim. As long as we are on the same wavelength, it's all good."

"We are. I swear it."

Chapter 11

Bas watched as the Lyft driver pulled out of the driveway with Lyra and Asim in the back seat. Since Bas drove them to his place at Asim's request, and Lyra called Henry to tell him where to pick up his RAV4, the only transportation available was calling for a car. Bas felt the two needed time for everything Asim needed to tell her.

Once they were out of sight, he headed back inside and looked around at the mess. She had gotten a bit rambunctious while she was undergoing her change, as Asim called it. Thankfully, the damage was minimal, but it would take him time to clean up. Pulling out a broom and dust pan, sweeping up the broken bits of furniture and knick-knacks was as good of a place to start as any.

After he swept the house out and took out the garbage, he headed to the bedroom to change the sheets, throwing out the ones now torn. He'd have to add new pillows to the list he was compiling, as well. Once the sheets were thrown out and the bed made, he headed to the kitchen to clean the dishes from breakfast. As he filled the sink with suds, a knock on his door stopped him. Drying his hands with a dish towel, he headed to see who his visitor might be, surprised since no one had ever come here before.

His surprise turned to shock when he opened the door to see Ma'at standing on his porch. His mouth went dry at seeing her there, yet his heart quickened as well.

"They're not here."

"I wasn't looking for them. Asim accomplished his mission and my sacred plume is now safe once again." Ma'at looked past him before she met his eyes. "Won't you invite me in, or is that no longer done in this century?"

Bas stammered and stepped back. "No. No. Of course, come in. I'm just surprised to see you here and figured you were looking for Asim."

She gracefully glided past him, looking around the interior. Once in the middle of the room, she turned back to face him. "Understandable. It would be the logical reason for my appearance. Truth is, I came for you."

Again, he was taken aback. "Why?" It was all he could manage to say. His mind came up with a dozen scenarios, but he was sure the one he really hoped for would be the most ludicrous.

"I find you intriguing. You barely seemed to care who I was. I appreciated not being worshipped at the mere mention of my name. It gets redundant after centuries of being revered. You also weren't afraid of me, willing to fight then assist me. It was refreshing, to say the least. Now, the danger has passed and I'm able to appreciate your efforts on my behalf. I'd like to indulge myself with you further."

Bas listened, but his eyes were trained solely on her. He remained quiet for a few moments, trying to comprehend what she was saying, and for him, it didn't sound quite as pleasing as she was trying to make it. He was a lot of things, but a goddess's boy toy was not on his list. He was never one for casual sex or casual anything.

"That's flattering, I'm sure, but it's not really my style."

"You're turning me down?" It was Ma'at's turn to be surprised. Who in their right mind would turn down a goddess?

"I'm really not one for casualness, though I think you're a beautiful woman. I've spent my life studying you and the others in your pantheon. I know what you can do and what you control, and I'm flattered you wish to be with me physically. I'm probably the biggest fool around for turning this down, but I'm interested in more than just sex."

She moved closer to him, placing her hand on his chest over his heart. Her eyes glowed a golden color before she pulled back. In that one touch, she saw and felt so much; she stared up at him in shock. "I agree to your terms."

Bas blinked and shook his head as if trying to empty it of cobwebs. "My terms?"

She gave him a wry smile. "I saw your heart, your wish and your desire. I saw who you were and who you'll become. I know you find me compelling, but you aren't sure why. I know you wish to have more than just sex, but rather a commitment with someone who cares about you as much as you care about them. I know you love Lyra, but it was better as someone you love like a sister, not a lover, even though you felt safe with her and looked no further. I know you and Lyra never quite worked because something was missing. At least until you met me. I've occupied your thoughts and you're unsure why. I am what you were missing. I'm not bragging, I can just see it more clearly and I understand what your future holds. I know what you want and I'm willing to try and give it to you. I have my duties, those won't change, but I also have a good deal of time I can spend with you and get to know who you are. I'd like to try, hence your terms."

Was this real? Was he dreaming? Did she really mean what she was telling him? She seemed to sense his hesitation as she stepped up to him, reaching around to pull him down to her level. Her lips were close to his as she whispered softly, "It's not a dream. I'd like for us to try."

Bas didn't care anymore. She was willing to give him what he wanted, and he couldn't resist her any further. He was under her spell, for better or worse. He closed the gap, letting his lips explore hers.

Chapter 12

Lyra looked around the now-empty apartment. A knock disturbed her momentary reverie, and she opened the door to find Bas and Asim standing shoulder to shoulder. Stepping back, she let them both enter. Bas moved to her and hugged her tight. "Are you sure this is what you want to do?"

"Yes. Besides, you get to move up in the world and take my position at the museum. And, with Ma'at staying with you, I feel like a third wheel. You two need time to yourselves without me hanging around. Being with a woman is hard enough, she is a goddess and is going to take a lot more of your time." Although she hadn't met the goddess personally, Bas had done nothing but talk about her incessantly every time they were together at work over the past week. A part of her wondered about the goddess who captured Bas' heart, but as long as he was happy, she was happy. It was all she ever wanted for him and he deserved someone to love who also loved him, even if it seemed to her like an odd pairing. Then again, she wanted to be with Asim, which was no stranger than Bas and Ma'at.

"I didn't want to get your job this way. I'd have happily been your assistant for many more years. As for Ma'at, she is trying to get used to the human world and I'm enjoying the opportunity to show it off. She reminds me a lot of you, and yet, there is something about her which I can't seem to resist. Admittedly, I'm not trying very hard. However, that said, I do worry about you. I'll never stop loving you."

"I know. I appreciate it more than words can say. I can't imagine a day without you in it. You've always been by my side. And you know how I am about major changes in my life. However, the E.M.A. has asked for everything we found to be returned. They don't trust we can continue to keep it safe, considering the break in and theft. Some of the pieces were damaged while they searched for the feather. Besides, I've got to be with Namire. With her artifacts. They'll let me head the research in documenting everything, and I'll need you to verify my findings. So, though I won't be with you physically, I'll be able to see you every day with video chats to discuss our findings. And you will be coming to Egypt every now and again, just as I'll come back here, so it's not goodbye, just see you later."

Asim knew additional times they could get together should they so desire, but he said nothing, letting the two of them say their goodbyes. In time he would explain everything, including all of her new-found powers. He had to smile to himself, knowing when she learned what she'd soon be able to accomplish would surprise her immensely. Hopefully, in a good way.

Bas pulled her into his arms again. "You've no idea how much I'm going to miss you."

"And I, you."

Bas let her go after squeezing her in a tight bear hug. He knew she hated change, but at this moment, he detested it as well. He lifted his chin, clenching his jaw as he turned around to face Asim. "You take real good care of her, 'cause if you don't, I don't care the cost, I'll hunt you down and kill you myself."

"I've no intention of allowing any harm to come to her," Asim quietly stated.

Bas gave a curt nod and strode out the door without a backward glance. He couldn't. They had been friends since college and together they had been through several shared lifetimes. He found it hard to imagine not being with her every day, even though a part of him was excited for the time he now had available for Ma'at. Since she met him at his cabin, they had been almost inseparable. She was so interested in learning the ways of the world and he was pleased to be educating her. But time spent with Ma'at and work wouldn't ease the pain of Lyra not being there.

"You got everything?" Asim closed the door after Bas departed, affording them a bit of privacy.

"Most is in storage. I had a few things shipped. They won't get there for about a week or so. I just have my suitcase, which is sufficient for now."

"Are you ready?" Asim reached for the suitcase, holding his free hand out to her.

Lyra placed her hand in his and nodded. "I'm ready."

"Once you're settled in, we'll need to have a serious discussion." He didn't wait for a response before he flashed her to his abode. Although it was only slightly better than when Namire had been there centuries ago, he'd made sure it was clean and as presentable as possible.

She was astonished. "How did you do that?"

"As long as I've been somewhere before, I have the ability to return immediately. It's an ability you will soon have too, once you hone the skill. It will make visiting Bas much easier. I would've told you earlier, but I didn't want to spoil the surprise. I truly meant it when I told you not to worry about leaving him or anyone else behind. You'll have the ability to visit them or bring them to you whenever you want, instantaneously. You'll be able to do that and so much more." Asim set her case down on the floor and looked around. With her here, it looked even more depressing than he originally thought. "I know it's not the most elaborate place you should be, but you can fix it up any way you wish. Namire said it only needed a woman's touch, but without a woman, I was fine with it. If you prefer a hotel until I can make it more presentable, I'll understand."

"You're talking to a woman who spends a portion of her life in a tent on a dig sight. This is luxurious by comparison."

"Lyra. I need to tell you something. I didn't want to tell you sooner because I didn't want it to influence your decision to come stay with me. To be with me."

Those words concerned her. What could he say that would make her consider any differently than the choice she had made to come here. "What is it?"

Asim wasn't sure how to break the news to her, so he chose to do it slowly. "Namire was the only other person I've ever had here. Although we were only together for a very short time, I loved her. I wanted to take care of her and protect her. I wanted a life with her and she agreed to a common law marriage." He knew he didn't need to explain what that was, since they had already discussed it earlier and she was knowledgeable in the old ways where a man and woman agreed to move in together and would be considered married without the need for a ceremony.

Lyra didn't know where this was going and, so far, she wasn't sure what to think. She only knew that he was telling her what he felt she needed to know slowly, in anticipation of whatever the shocking news entailed.

"I know you wondered how I could care so deeply for you when we've just met. I'm not sure if I mentioned it or not, but you remind me of her."

Lyra smiled and was about to say how sweet it was, but he gestured for her to remain silent, then took both her hands in his. He stared down at their interlocked fingers, his thumb rubbing softly over her knuckles. He was quiet for several minutes, but she waited patiently, knowing he'd tell her when he was ready.

"The reason why we're so connected to each other is because you're Namire reincarnated."

She laughed, feeling it was a joke, but when he didn't meet her gaze and she could feel how serious he was, she sobered. "So, it's not me you love, but who you think I used to be in a past life?" She pulled her hands away. She was confused, uncertain. She wanted to be loved for who she was, not who she might have been in some other life centuries ago.

"No. That's not what I meant. That's not how it works. Reincarnation is the essence of a person returning to life in search of their soulmate, so they can be happy. Sometimes it's because they were torn apart too soon, like Namire was. Sometimes it's just another way to complete whatever journey they'd set upon before one or both passed. And sometimes it's just a love so profound, that it'll keep being reborn to search out the soul meant for them."

"You're kidding me, right?"

"No. Reincarnation exists. I'm too old to not have seen all the wonders of this world and that's one of the miracles the gods have bestowed upon us. You're Namire. Anubis confirmed it." He sighed. He wanted to reach for her again, but since she pulled away, he respected her wishes. "I've fallen in love with you for you. For who you are now. Your strength, your adaptability, your intelligence. I'm only saying that my ka has been searching for you and it recognized you even before my conscious self was able to. Reincarnation only opened the way for us to find each other again and restore the connection we once had. Knowing you were once Namire doesn't change how I feel about you as Lyra."

"How long have you known? Always?"

"No. I felt the connection, but I didn't understand it. When you were dying, Anubis confirmed it. He told me after I saved you. He wanted me to rescue you not because I knew who you once were, but for who you are now. Although he didn't understand why I hadn't figured it out on my own. I think a part of me couldn't believe it was possible."

"And you waited to tell me this, why?"

"I didn't know how you felt. I didn't know if you were in love with Bas, or if you detested who and what I was. Maybe age would've been a factor, or any other multitude of reasons why you were no longer interested. I was also concerned because of what I did to you. If you wanted nothing more to do with me because I turned you without your permission."

She frowned. "You changed me to save my life. I'm not a fool that I don't understand this. You had no choice. I surely would've died had you not intervened. I've got a lot to get used to, a great number of new abilities I need to develop. I returned to Egypt with you because you can teach me all I need to learn. I came because this is where Namire is, since the E.M.A. took her back. Now you're saying I came because, what? I've got to be with you because of who I once was? That my decisions aren't my own? That I'm following some pre-ordained destiny? I don't believe in any of that. I came here because of my choices. I've worked very hard to find Namire and I'm not letting some bureaucracy take me away from my life's work."

Asim stepped back as if she'd slapped him across the face. She didn't care for him. She just used him for sex, needed him to train her for her new life, and wanted nothing more from him. How could he have been so gullible? "I understand. You are welcome to continue to use this place. I'm rarely here anyway. I won't disturb you. Call me when you are ready for guidance with your powers or for anything else."

Lyra appeared shocked, her eyebrows raised in astonishment. "You're just going to leave? I never said I wanted you to go anywhere. You sprung this on me like it was nothing more than saying you just baked chocolate chip cookies. Give me a chance to process this new revelation before you go gallivanting off, leaving me alone."

"I don't bake."

"It was a simile. Asim, the idea of mystical creatures, actual gods and goddesses, and powers, which I'm totally lost in how to use, is against my belief. I never dreamed any of this existed. I never believed in being able to shift from human to animal, or transport from one place to another across the world in the blink of an eye. Now you're telling me reincarnation exists and I'm one of those reincarnated. This is a lot of information for just a few hours or even a couple of weeks."

He didn't totally agree, but he didn't have a chance to respond as a bright golden light blinded them both. When they could see again, Ma'at was standing before them. Asim bowed quickly, tugging Lyra to follow suit. She didn't understand what had just happened, who this woman was, nor why she was here, but she bowed anyway.

"Don't bow to me, child. Asim, you may also rise."

Ma'at began to walk around the two-room structure, every now and again swiping a shelf or piece of furniture as if to check for dirt.

Lyra mouthed "Who?" but Asim shook his head so she remained quiet and waited.

"This won't do for my descendant." Another

blinding light and the structure was altered into a two-story home, complete with marble floors, ornate furnishings, and rich mahogany woodwork.

"Your descendant?" Lyra looked back and forth between the woman and Asim. She could tell the latter had no idea she was related to this woman, somehow, from the total shock displayed upon his features.

"Lyra, this is the goddess Ma'at."

"You're Ma'at? How?" Lyra was speechless. She was still processing the fact she was now a jackal. Then the news she is the reincarnation of Namire, and now she finds out she's not only in the presence of a goddess, but is related to her? Her knees suddenly felt like jelly. Asim moved behind Lyra to help steady her, sensing her weakness caused by so many monumental revelations.

"I wasn't sure when I saw you on the sacrificial table, so after I made sure my feather was safe, I did some research. I believe you're called Mayet? Bas was able to fill in a few blanks as well. I hope you don't mind his talking about you. He doesn't fully understand yet that you and I are related. Honestly, it surprised me as well. I can tell you are the reincarnation of Namire from your ka, but to be related to me as well is a surprise."

Lyra could only nod, unsure where the lump in her throat appeared from but preventing her from vocalizations of any kind. At least anything resembling her own voice. The one word she managed to squeak out sounded like it came from a frog. "How?"

"Very good question. Ages ago, I had a son by

Thoth, the god of wisdom and once my husband. Our son, Mahet, consorted with Great Wife of Pharaoh Ramses II. Since he bore 94 children, he didn't realize the 95th was sired by my son. As the years progressed, the son of my son's son realized who truly sired him and took the name Mayet. Mayet is what Ma'at was altered from, to protect my family. You bear my name. You're of my blood. When Namire's time to be reborn came, her ka realized whose bloodline she needed to be a part of in order to find Asim. It was all predicted and has now come to pass."

Asim helped Lyra to a chair to sit. This was something even he didn't know. He was as surprised as she was.

"I can see this has come as a shock to you." Ma'at stood regally still, her gaze remaining on Lyra. "You've got quite a lot of information to digest, so I'll leave you for now. When you've come to terms and are ready to ask the multitude of questions I'm sure you'll have, Asim or Bas knows how to contact me. We'll have a nice discussion over tea. In the meantime, I'll know you're in a place worthy of your status."

As goddesses tended to do, she shimmered away in a blindingly golden light, leaving Lyra and Asim alone. Asim gazed around the enhanced abode. What once had been his comfortable shack was not quite a palace, but far more elaborate than he could ever have made it.

Lyra looked up at him. "Do you still want me?"

He swung his head around, then squatted next to her to be more level. "Why would you ever think

I wouldn't? Lyra, you're still you. Being the reincarnation of the woman I loved just made it easier to love you, but it's still you. Being related to a powerful goddess doesn't change who you are inside. My soul found yours because they're meant to be together. However, you still have free will. If you don't want to be with me, I'll respect your decision. But, me still wanting you? Every moment of every day I want to hold you, kiss you, make love to you. You make me whole. I've never realized how much I was missing until you entered my life. Yes, I loved Namire. I always have from the moment I first met her, but all that did was open my heart up to you when I first saw you. You embody her spirit, but you outshine her memory."

"So, that's a yes?"

He chuckled. "That's a yes. I'm in love with Lyra Mayet. Everything else you might be, is just an adventure."

She took a moment to digest everything, then leaned forward to whisper against his lips. "Show me."

Without another word, he scooped her up off the chair and carried her into the bedroom.

ABOUT THE AUTHOR

Ms. Hawks has always been interested in writing in some form or other. Several years ago, she was involved with and then ran a Star Trek Interactive Writing Group, which was successful for a number of years. Yes, she is a trekker and proud of it.

A few years back, she received her Master's Degree in Ancient Civilizations, Native American History, and United States History.

She lives in the suburbs of Chicago with her three companions, all males—cats. She travels as much as she can to various Author/Reader conventions and loves to meet established fans and make new ones, some of whom she considers friends more than fans.

Check her out on her website: Laura-Hawks.com

MORE FROM LAURA HAWKS

Demon Trilogy

LAURA HAWKS

Spirit Walker's Saga

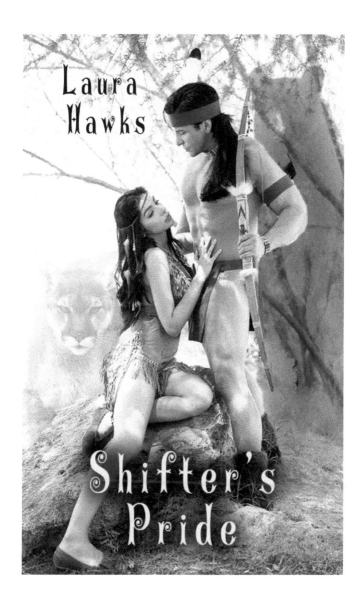

Paranormal Ghosts

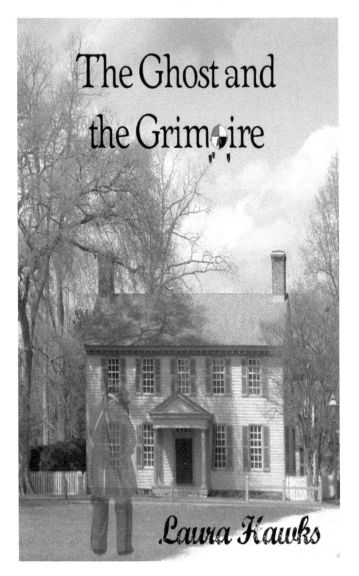

The Ghost and
the Grimoire

Laura Hawks

Shatter Fairytales

Laura Hawks

Snow White
and the
Seven Cannibals

Contemporary Suspense/Thriller